DEFENDING THE LOST

DEFENDING THE LOST

RECLAIMING HONOR™ BOOK 6

JUSTIN SLOAN

MICHAEL ANDERLE

DISRUPTIVE IMAGINATION®

DEFENDING THE LOST (this book) is a work of fiction.

All of the characters, organizations, and events portrayed in this novel are either products of the author's imagination or are used fictitiously. Sometimes both.

Copyright © 2017 Justin Sloan and Michael T. Anderle
Cover by Mario Wibisono
https://www.artstation.com/artist/mario_wibisono

Cover copyright © LMBPN Publishing

LMBPN Publishing supports the right to free expression and the value of copyright. The purpose of copyright is to encourage writers and artists to produce the creative works that enrich our culture.

The distribution of this book without permission is a theft of the author's intellectual property. If you would like permission to use material from the book (other than for review purposes), please contact info@kurtherianbooks.com. Thank you for your support of the author's rights.

LMBPN Publishing
PMB 196, 2540 South Maryland Pkwy
Las Vegas, NV 89109

First US edition, August, 2017
Version 1.01, October 2018

The Kurtherian Gambit (and what happens within / characters / situations / worlds) are copyright © 2017 by Michael T. Anderle.

From Justin

To Ugulay, Verona and Brendan Sloan

From Michael

To Family, Friends and
Those Who Love
To Read.
May We All Enjoy Grace
To Live The Life We Are
Called.

DEFENDING THE LOST TEAM

JIT Beta Readers

Kelly ODonnell
James Caplan
Erika Daly
Joshua Ahles
Kimberly Boyer
Melissa OHanlon
Peter Manis
Paul Westman
Micky Cocker
Thomas Ogden

If we missed anyone, please let us know!

Editor

Lynne Stiegler

Thank you to the following Special Consultants

Jeff Morris - US Army - Asst Professor Cyber-Warfare, Nuclear Munitions (Active)
W.W.D.E

CHAPTER ONE

Outside Toro

Robin paced the deck of the airship, ignoring the recently recruited pirate slaves and even the occasional glance from Valerie. All she could think about was that they were rapidly approaching Toro, the place where she hoped she could liberate her parents from captivity.

A memory kept flashing through her mind, incessantly harassing her. That night when the vampires had come.

It had been a peaceful night, one spent listening to her dad go on about his plans for them.

"When we're through this and we've settled down," he had said, "we'll have the biggest house this side of Chicago. That's what I'll build for you. There will be grand windows with a view of the mountains so you'll always have something to inspire you when you're painting, dear."

At the time she had loved the idea, since she was always painting when not out gathering berries or helping her dad hunt. Now it was different; painting seemed like the stupidest waste of time.

"We don't need a big house," her mom had countered,

lowering herself to the log he sat on and wrapping her arms around him. "Just one that keeps us together and warm."

"As long as it will give you two some privacy," Robin had joked, flicking a small twig at them. "Keep it clean."

"Robin!" Her mom gave her a scolding look. "You should be happy your parents still love each other."

"She should be happy we're both alive, given this hellhole of a world," her dad had said, voice raspy.

It was the first time she heard him talk so negatively, as well as the first time she'd seen that look in his eyes—terror.

Her mom had given her a glance that said, "Not now," and soon they had gone to bed in their one-room shack. Robin laid there staring at the two of them, wondering what had spooked her dad so. She promised herself she would find out in the morning.

Except that morning had never come. Not really, anyway. Just as she was nodding off, the front door had been kicked in by a man with glowing red eyes and then two more had swept in with such speed and power she was sure they were demons.

It hadn't taken long for her to discover they were vampires. They had soon made her one of their own and sent her mom and dad off to be sold as slaves.

There had been so much screaming, shouting, and struggling that night. She remembered the smell of piss, though she didn't think it came from her, and something gripping her arms so tightly she had thought it was all over.

But the image that really kept haunting her was the terror in her father's eyes before they had gone to bed. That loss of hope.

She couldn't shake it from her mind, no matter how hard she tried. No matter what sort of distractions she put in its place.

"Robin," a voice called, and she looked up to see Valerie giving her a worried and caring smile. "We're here. We're landing right now. Are you ready?"

Without so much as a nod, she turned and looked at the blur

of the city that was just starting to come into view. Was she ready to save her parents and bring a level of revenge to this city that they had likely never seen?

Hell, yes, she was!

It worried Valerie that Robin was so distant and quiet, but she understood. If it were the other way around—if Valerie thought there was the slightest chance of saving her family—she would already have charged in and slaughtered every one of those bastards by this point.

They had secured their small armada of blimps on the far side of a hill that separated them from Toro, so that they would go unseen by the pirates. Now Valerie stood close to the peak, waiting and watching as a woman approached—a scout, it seemed.

The woman had on a long black coat over torn jeans and a ragged shirt with a bandana tied around her head and a brimmed hat to keep the sun from her eyes, likely so that she'd be a better shot with the old AK-47 she carried. Valerie cocked her head at the sight of that, wondering if its presence meant they were manufacturing ammunition here. That could be of use, when this was all over.

She waited in the cover of some tall grass until the woman was nearly upon them, then moved with vampire speed to sweep the woman's legs out from under her and snatch the rifle. Her next action was to crouch and aim the rifle at the scout's face.

"You're with us or against us," Valerie barked, nodding to Robin, who looked like a ninja, and the others behind her.

The woman's eyes narrowed and she pulled a blade from her side, swinging for Valerie's throat.

Bad move.

Valerie moved aside on instinct and slammed the butt of the

rifle into the woman's nose hard. Possibly a little *too* hard, as it didn't just break her nose but caved her face in.

The scout gave a half-dying, crazed scream as blood gushed and the bone likely lodged in her brain took its time cutting off life. Valerie realized she now had no choice. She dropped the rifle and covered the woman's mouth with one hand while snatching the knife and slitting her throat with the other.

The vampire waited until she stopped twitching.

Responding to a wave of her hand, Martha and River ran up and dragged the body back over the hill behind them.

Dammit! Blood covered the hand that had been on the woman's mouth and she sniffed it, contemplating. Not long ago she would have been all over that blood to absorb the nanocytes within, but with Michael's energy flowing through her now, she didn't need it.

She positioned herself to watch the city, hating herself right then for being forced to take a life, and not wanting to make eye contact with any of the others.

Old Toronto, they called the city, and now that Valerie knew where it was and where Robin's parents were likely being held, it pissed her off. They had done well by going north first, following the coast to deal with the pirates who had been interrupting trade with what remained of Europe. Cammie and Royland had taken over from the character who had styled himself "the Prince" before Valerie and Robin had beaten him into a bloody pulp.

Now that the coast was taken care of, however, it was time to rid the continent of the rest of these jackholes. Apparently that meant heading inland to an area not far from where they had traveled when moving through Ohio to Chicago, according to Valerie's estimations on flying distance and directions.

If she had known that then, she would have simply gone north, killed everyone, and been done with it.

Of course, proper maps didn't exist now, and that was probably for the best. Since she had been talking to the slaves they had rescued from Slaver's Peak, she had a better understanding of the situation. These people weren't all bad. In fact, many of them were just trying to survive. They were no different from the people of Old Manhattan before Valerie helped liberate them.

Here she was, staring down at a city that didn't appear to be so different from New York, and she had a whole new group of people to liberate.

"Tell me," she said, glancing over at the man named Rand, whom she had grown to trust in the days since the fight at Slaver's Peak, "where would the council meet? There?"

She pointed to a dome on the far side of the city, closer to the lake. The large spike of a building or monument—she wasn't sure which—stood next to it, with several toppled buildings nearby. The city was in much better shape than New York, with more infrastructure intact on the outskirts of the city. There was also a section of it that was clearly segregated from the rest; she could see that even from here. People had set up obstacles, spikes with concertina wire, and other barriers that would stop any sort of assault.

The needle and the dome were within that area, but Rand shook his head.

"The slaves will likely be in that area, but not in the dome," he told them. "They held sporting events and whatnot there back in the day. Wouldn't make sense to use it as a stronghold, not with the crazies in the world now."

"What do you know?" Robin glared at him, and Valerie had to laugh, remembering that Robin's assassin trainers had headquartered them in a converted sports arena.

Why she was getting defensive about the idea was beyond Valerie.

Rand just snorted. "Used to live *there*, in the slums." He motioned to a bend on the other side of the lake. "That area was hit hard in the riots, and it's now mostly cardboard houses. When

I was taken, that's where I was, and when we free this city, that's the first place I'm going."

"You'd live in a cardboard box?" Martha asked. "There are surely better options."

She and River stood behind them, staying below the sight of any possible lookouts from the city.

"Not to live there," Rand replied. "To find out what happened to my sister. If they touched her, you all will have a hard time holding me back."

"Holding you back?" Robin started to stand. "As far as we know my parents are being held as slaves in this city. I say we go in now, guns blazing!"

Valerie put a hand on her arm and shook her head. "There are too many innocents."

She wished she could see Robin's expression under the black assassin's mask she wore along with her other protective clothing to shield her from exposure to sunlight. The sun was at full strength, hovering just past midday.

"Like my sister," Rand agreed. "She's never done a thing wrong in her life, just tries to make it from one day to the next."

A glance over her shoulder showed Valerie the other men and women, those they had rescued from Slaver's Peak and who would have otherwise been forced into the life of piracy, preparing the airships and loading weapons in case she gave the order to assault the city.

When she thought of the way the Prince had treated his people, shooting the community with bullets from an airship Gatling gun and worse, her eyes glowed red and she wanted nothing more than to charge into this city and tear it to shreds. But Rand had a point.

All her friends from New York would be dead right now if she had started a killing spree on arrival. A thought hit her and she frowned. When had killing become such a common thing?

Like that woman, the scout or guard or whatever. Instinct had taken over, not even leaving a moment for doubt.

When she had first arrived in New York, taking a life had felt like an egregious sin. Now she found herself teetering on the edge of the "greater good" argument.

If past Valerie could read present Valerie's mind, she would slap the stupidity right out of her.

Present Valerie knew she shouldn't cross that line. On the other side waited only darkness.

"Rand's right," she finally agreed, imagining the glare Robin was probably giving her. "We're going to find your parents, I promise. But we're going to do so with the fewest possible casualties." When Robin said nothing, Valerie added, "Imagine if we attacked and innocents were killed in the fight, people used as cannon fodder or hostages during the siege. Now imagine you're walking through the streets of Toro afterwards and the dead are lying there with blank stares—and among them are your parents."

"Shut up," Robin hissed, pulling her arm away. "I'm not arguing with you. I'm waiting patiently for you to come up with a plan that doesn't suck."

Valerie smiled. "I think I just did."

The others waited, and Rand got a nervous look on his face. "Don't say it."

"Well, we have a person here who knows at least one area of this city fairly well," she replied, giving Rand a look that said he had no choice. "We go in through the slums. Get close, find out what we can, and then make our move."

"It's not going to be easy," he told them. "I mean, I knew the streets when I lived there. I knew who was who, but then they started patrols. They started corralling us, shipping us off to Slaver's Peak, or worse."

"Do you still know your way around?"

He shrugged. "I mean, yeah, it's not like it has been *that* long."

"Good." She moved away from the hillcrest and motioned for the others to follow. "Gather everyone and set up a secure location for now. Just a few of us will go in with Rand. We'll keep it small until we know what we're dealing with."

The others nodded and got to it, leaving Valerie to pause and look back at that needle-like building sticking up into the air. Perhaps it had once been a thing of beauty, a symbol of God-knew-what, but now it was like a spear or a sword's tip, reminding her that people were going to die during this assault one way or another.

She would just have to do her best to ensure it was only the bad people.

CHAPTER TWO

Prince Edward Island

Cammie had been on the island for a few days now, but she still felt her nerves act up when she had to go out and talk to the people. She lingered in the doorway, looking back at Royland and considering how glad she was that he was here with her.

In another version of their reality, one where Valerie would have tasked her alone to take charge of this former pirate group, she would likely have torn them all to shreds by now. Well, maybe not all of them, but the ones who looked at her funny. And that had been a damn lot of them.

"Do you have to go?" Royland asked from the table where he sat looking out at the sunlight sparkling on the water. She knew he longed to walk outside freely during the day, but she would trade that for his speed and power any time.

"It's our duty now, isn't it?" she replied. "They say the guy was caught breaking into her house with a knife in his hands."

"But we don't know who to trust here."

She nodded. "That's the role we've stepped into. These people have been told they need to rob and steal to survive, and that murder is okay if it helps you get ahead."

"Are we any different?"

"Seriously?" She stared at him, then rolled her eyes when she saw the smile pull at his lips. "That's what I thought."

He stood and approached her, but stopped where the sunlight came in through the doorway. "We were like them once though, weren't we? I mean, I know I sure as hell was."

Cammie turned away at that, flushing.

"I didn't mean—"

"No, I know you didn't." She stood there for a moment, unable to wrench her mind away from the memories the comment had brought up. She had been a hunter of vampires at one point, and before that she had been with the Golden City Weres. She certainly couldn't call herself innocent in any regard.

"The point is, none of us are guiltless these days," he explained. "And that's what makes this world so tough to figure out."

"But us especially. Our past is what makes us capable though, isn't it?" She turned to him, hopeful. "I mean, we've lived the dark path, so we know where it can lead and what it means to escape. What it means to be honorable."

"We have to guide them," he agreed, nodding. He reached a hand almost into the sunlight, and she took it. Giving it a squeeze, she leaned in and kissed him, then said, "Don't wait up."

He chuckled. "I'll be in my coffin."

She laughed at that, glad to have a reason to push away the negativity. Vampires didn't really sleep in coffins—or at least she didn't think so.

Heading outside, she ducked under the streaming flag she had hung outside the door. It was blowing so hard in the wind that it nearly whipped her face. Good thing she had those Were reflexes.

She pulled the cloth back, tucking it into the scrunchie she had wrapped around the pole to hold the flag down on windy days, then paused, looking at the symbol on it: a crown on a skull.

It had been the Prince's symbol and was his flag, given to them once he was out of the picture to indicate who was in charge.

It didn't sit right with her though, associating herself with that monster. If they were going to bring change to this place, the imagery needed to be fresh. With a growl she tore the flag off the pole, tucked it into the pocket of her long pirate jacket, and made her way down the steps.

The house wasn't large, but it had been built in the days before the great collapse. Not everyone here enjoyed such luxury; many lived in plywood shacks, and some of the really drugged-out ones preferred the streets. At least it was warm enough nowadays.

A crowd was already gathering by the square, the same area where Valerie had, just days before, stood up for a man and rescued his wife's corpse. Damn, this place had its depressing side. Cammie hoped to the gods or whatever was out there that the bastards who had done that to the poor man had left with the Prince and were now bleeding out on the side of a road somewhere.

There wasn't a doubt in her mind that Valerie had dealt with the Prince and his followers. What worried her was Valerie's eagerness to trust people; to believe they could start over.

It had certainly worked in Cammie's favor, but that didn't mean she wanted to be standing next to a bunch of converted pirates and hoping they would have her back in a fight.

Several of the women glared at her as she approached, but then she noticed a pointed look from one of them accompanied by a quick glance upward. A stutter-step later Cammie gave her a slight nod of appreciation before she turned to sniff.

Yup, there was someone up there. By the smell of it, someone who hadn't bathed in years. She wasn't sure if she should be thankful for the Were sense of smell for possibly saving her life or annoyed at it for gifting her with that horrible stench.

Perking her ears, she waited, focusing on that spot above and drowning out the chatter ahead, then heard movement.

She moved first, sidestepping into the cover of a nearby shack, then drew her pistol and shot.

The man fell, landed head-first, and didn't move again.

Cammie shook her head, then turned to see everyone silent and staring at her.

"This keeps up, how many of you will be left?" she demanded, marching into their midst.

"Most of us, I'd imagine," a young man with a red mustache told her. "Seeing as most of us mean you no harm."

Her heart was thumping and she had wanted an excuse to snap at someone, but this man surprised her. Either he was genuine and she'd need him close by so that he could keep an eye out for her, or he was full of it and she'd need him close by for her to keep an eye on.

"And you are?" she asked.

"William," he replied, then gestured to three men and two women behind him. "This is my crew. Every one of us is loyal to the teeth. We've been talking around here, speaking with the others, you know. As I said, most have your back. You don't take shit, but you don't give it out unwarranted neither."

She nodded, liking this man more by the second. "We're changing this place, and I see a role for you in the new system."

William's eyes narrowed, but he tilted his head and asked, "Changing it how?"

"For starters," she turned to the rest of the crowd, another thirty folks or so, she guessed, "we're not pirates anymore, though you've heard that before. Privateers, maybe? That works. From now on, I want you to think of this community as Valerie's Navy."

"You're the leader here," William confirmed. "We follow you."

She nodded. "I appreciate that, but here's the truth: I follow Valerie, so anything you do for me, you do for her."

William glanced at his companions, then nodded. "Agreed."

"I'm your captain and this whole island is a boat. We need to steer this boat in the right direction, so I'm going to need your help."

"You're still unproven," a woman from the other side of the square called. She was short, long hair in a bun, and looked to be in her late forties. "I've got no problem following a new captain if I know there's treasure on the other side."

Cammie nodded. She got this woman. "You want treasure? How about a life without violence? No more bloodshed, no more friends and loved ones dying. That's what we're bringing about down in New York, and that's what we'll bring here. But it takes work."

"Peace?" The woman scoffed. "I talk of treasure and you offer us peace?"

Cammie glanced around, noticing general agreement with the woman from all but William and his crew, who seemed to be amused by the discussion.

"How about this?" Cammie offered, stepping toward her. "Would you say there are other pirates out there? Other bandits, cutthroats, murderers?"

The woman laughed. "Of course."

"And if we were to become the force that takes them down? A police force, perhaps, that stops them, and if we can't find who their loot belongs to, we take it for our treasure?"

She could see the woman's mind working, her smile forming. "You mean we get treasure *and* we get to look at our kids with pride in our eyes?"

"That's the idea."

"Sold." The woman took two long strides over and shook Cammie's hand. "The name's Platea, and I'm with you on one condition. You keep killing assholes like him when warranted." She motioned to the dead man on the street, the one Cammie had just shot.

But Cammie's eyes moved to the man glaring at her, the one tied to a beam of wood the community had erected in the center of the square.

"You mean like this man?" she asked Platea.

"Guess whose daughter's room the bastard was trying to enter?" Platea snarled, turning her gaze to the man as her eyes glazed with hatred. "Guess whose daughter he would have had his way with if a certain someone named Platea hadn't torn him from there and dragged him into the street?"

"That's your story, bitch," the man growled, spitting at her feet.

"And what's yours?" Cammie asked.

Platea opened her mouth, but Cammie held up a hand. "Let him speak."

Murmurs rose from the crowd, giving Cammie the feeling that trials hadn't really been all that common under the Prince. It had likely been more of an "accuse and then kill" situation. Probably the one who annoyed the Prince more was the one who got killed. Well, not anymore.

The man looked doubtful, then sneered. "Way it happened was the girl told me she was going to pay me, in the market. Bought a sword, and when I asked what sort of payment she meant...well, let's just say the look she gave me was unmistakable. Imagine my surprise when I followed her around the corner and she was gone. So yes, I naturally came to collect my payment."

Cammie cocked her head, licked her lips, and laughed. "You mean you gave her the sword without any actual verbal contract for...the sexual favors you were owed, and then thought you'd force yourself on her to collect? Did I really just hear you right?"

The man's color drained at the look she was giving him, but he clenched his jaw. "I required payment."

Cammie rubbed her temples, considering this. It was almost too easy. There was the fact that he had clearly meant to rape this woman's daughter, though he had been stopped before succeeding. Then again, if he was going to do it once, he had likely done it before and would do it again.

And he seemed like the type who would be proud of it.

"Sir," she said, mockingly, "let me ask you this. How many women, no, girls, have you…collected payment from?"

He rolled his eyes. "I get what's mine, and this town knows it. You want to fuck with me, I fuck with you. That's right. Way I see it, you owe me for wasting my–"

Blood poured from his neck and Cammie, usually cavalier about sex and related things, stood over him with her knife in one hand and his hair in the other. He jerked, horrified eyes staring at her, and then went limp.

She dropped his head and it landed chin on his chest, then she turned to the crowd.

Some of their jaws hung open, but William just looked impressed. Platea smiled smugly.

"He got his trial," Cammie declared, turning to look each of them in the eye. "Would Valerie have handled it differently? Maybe. Would the Queen Bitch? I wish I knew, but I'll tell you one thing. Someone tries something like that, then brags about it and threatens me? Not going to fly on my ship. Not while I'm captain."

"We wouldn't have it any other way," William affirmed, and the rest of the crowd murmured its agreement.

"Great." Cammie wiped her blade on the dead man's clothes, then motioned to him and then the other body. "If everyone stays in line, this will not be a normal occurrence. I promise you that. Now, do we have any volunteers to clean up this mess?"

William only needed to look at his men before the three of them stepped forward and got to work. William approached her as Cammie was about to leave, one of the women he'd brought with him close behind.

"Allow me to introduce Brae," he said. "She's the most skilled sailor I've ever met. When do we mean to sail?"

"Sail?" Cammie asked, distractedly.

"You made some promises."

"Ah, yes." Cammie glanced back, noticing Platea talking with someone who must've been her daughter and saw the way the girl, no more than sixteen, was looking at her. If she wasn't mistaken, there was something that girl needed to tell her. "If you'll excuse me. Just ready the boats and ensure they're in top shape, but…not yet."

"As you wish." The two walked off.

When Cammie turned around from watching them go, Platea was there with her daughter.

"Clara has something to say." Platea turned to her daughter, who was waiting. "Go on, spit it out."

The girl, thin but with more muscle tone than Cammie would have thought when she first saw her, seemed shy at first. After a moment, however, it became clear that she was looking down and clenching her jaw out of some unexpected emotion. Rage?

"What's wrong, girl?" Cammie asked, not one to take this sort of behavior lightly.

"I should've been the one to slit his throat," Clara stated. "After doing much worse, I assure you."

"Tell her what you told me, and stop your whining," her mother ordered, whapping her a good one across the back. Clara glared, but didn't strike back or say anything to the woman.

"It might be better if we spoke in private." Clara's eyes darted to the other men and women, still loitering in the square or slowly making their way out.

"The gist, please," Cammie requested. "Then I'll decide if that's necessary."

"There was an attempted mutiny in Old Manhattan recently," Clara replied.

"New York now," Cammie muttered, then shook her head. "Wait, what? How would you know that?"

Clara leaned in now, voice quieter. "I was part of a group that served, er, your kind. I was part of it, but…"

"Go on," her mother hissed.

"I'm here to seek your pardon. To serve *you* now."

Cammie blinked, caught totally off guard by all this, and then nodded. "Yes, I think you're right about needing to discuss this in private. Come on." She nodded for them to follow, and the three made their way back to the house. Whatever this was, she needed to know what had happened in New York, and she needed to know what would happen next.

CHAPTER THREE

New York

Sandra leaned against the wall of Colonel Donnoly's office, a place she had begun to associate with stress and heartache. How many members of their new army had they lost because they hadn't seen Esmerelda and Presley's treachery coming? They had dipped their hands into the Colonel's cookie jar, and he had let them take every last crumb.

Yet somehow he sat at the front of the room, still in charge.

Diego sat beside Garcia and gave Sandra a look that said he knew what was going on in her mind. The conversation had come up several times over the last few days, and he had insisted that it couldn't be changed, that to throw out Donnoly now would be too upsetting to the system. Instead they would treat him like a puppet and be sure everyone was focused now, headed the right direction.

Also present were Felix, who represented the Weres, and Brad, who had quickly proven himself and now stood for the vampires.

"Our first strike team is ready," Brad was saying. "Each group is represented in both squads, and I've appointed the squad leaders personally."

"You've lead a raid of this magnitude?" Donnoly asked skeptically, then adjusted himself in his seat with an uncomfortable look.

"I've been part of them," Brad replied, glaring.

"And I've seen what the boy's capable of," Garcia offered. "I vouch for him."

Brad turned his glare on Garcia. "Thanks, but I'm not a boy."

"Hey, whether you've got the banana or the taco, I vouch for your military prowess, okay?"

Diego chuckled and Sandra rolled her eyes as he, Garcia, and Felix gave each other a slight nod—what the three had taken to calling a mental high-five. Ever since working together to help save the city, they had become best buds. Almost inseparable, much to her annoyance.

"I meant I'm a man, not a boy," Brad stated, and let his fangs show with a growl.

"A man knows when threats are necessary and when they're just plain stupid," Garcia replied, staring him down. "I was saying that I support you. Take the compliment or not, but either way, back the fuck up."

Now it was Sandra's turn to laugh. When Donnoly and Brad both turned to her, she shrugged. "Hey, he has a point, right?"

Donnoly nodded. "He had your back, Brad. And you're being a bit of a dick."

Even Brad laughed now, not used to Donnoly talking like that. "Fine, sorry. I've been a bit worked up."

"Hey, we all have." Donnoly held his hands out as if revealing he had nothing up his sleeves. "I'm not going to deny what happened. Come on, I let my…banana, is that what you said, Sergeant?" At a nod from Garcia, he continued, "I let my banana be my guide, you know. Two beautiful women, and I fell apart in their hands. You should all kick me out on the street, but," he held his hands up again, as if pushing a wall back this time, "here's the thing, you really shouldn't. You don't want to, and I don't want to go. Have I learned my lesson?"

He adjusted himself again in his seat as if something was itching, then seemed to lose his train of thought.

"Have you?" Sandra asked, trying not to smirk.

"Yes, of course I've learned my lesson," he finished, irritably. "The point is, we need to pull ourselves together. Stand united."

"Behind *you*?" Felix asked, his expression failing to hide what he thought of that idea. He ignored the look from Sandra as he continued. "There aren't many who doubt this whole mess was due to incompetence on your part."

Donnoly nodded and considered the large Were. "When things went sour here… The last time, I mean. Well, one of the many times. There was a reason the others stood behind me. Am I a military leader like Sergeant Garcia here? No. Am I the most strategic? I'm not. But I'm not corrupt, and now I've learned a very tough lesson about letting those around me get too close. I'd say I have taken in this lesson better than any of you, and in spite of the heavy bag of shame that has slammed down over me, I am willing to continue to serve the people of New York. But only with you all, the experts, at my side. If you want me gone, just say the word."

Felix thought about what the man had said, then leaned back, eyes moving to each person around the table. When they at last came to rest on Sandra, he nodded.

"We move forward as is," Sandra assured him. "And let me tell you what a relief it is for that to be out of the way. If there's one thing we can't spend time on, it's infighting. Squabbling and bickering will get us nowhere."

"Agreed," several muttered around the table.

"We strike back, and we strike with a vengeance," Donnoly declared, fist smacking the table in a show of determination that made Sandra want to laugh. But no, she was playing the supportive role, and he was right—his inability to hold himself together in the face of two beautiful women had been a tough lesson. She was going to trust that he had learned it and was back to his old self.

Although… She might send a test his way at some point. The idea amused her, and as far as she knew it was necessary. Something to keep in her back pocket, if nothing else.

"We'll brief the teams come morning," Garcia stated as he stood. "Send out the soldiers first to see what we're dealing with, then have the vamps and Weres ready to do the dirty work."

It wasn't that the non-modified humans couldn't get it done, Sandra knew. The fact that vampires and Weres could both heal and likely take out the enemy much faster just made using them for strikes the practical decision.

"Very well," Donnoly said, standing too, trying his best to not show he was uncomfortable. "Then let's put a period on this very long day and call it done."

The rest all stood and started to meander out.

"Oh, and Colonel?" Sandra walked past him and leaned in close. "All that itching, down there? You might want to stop by the infirmary to see if they have something for it."

"Er, yes, thank you." He stood, proud as ever, and walked to the elevator, moving his hips in an odd motion to avoid scratching as he went.

"Think he'll be okay?" Felix asked, standing at her shoulder.

"The soldiers respect him as one of their own," she replied. "Most of them, anyway. We'll help him earn the trust back from the rest, and keep close to ensure he doesn't muck all this up again."

"I've got some of my best on it." Felix turned to Diego and Garcia. "Now, boys—work hard, play hard?"

"You're speaking my language!" Garcia grinned. "To the café?"

"No way," Sandra interrupted, putting her foot down. "I might not be able to drink wine anymore, but the rest of New York won't be able to either if you lot keep getting into it. Plus, I'm still not convinced Felix here isn't trying to seduce my man."

Felix laughed at that. "Hey, I'd crush Diego in a hypothetical world, but such a world is sadly a dream." He reached out to caress Diego's cheek, stopping halfway. "Ah, the one that got away."

They all cracked up at that, and Diego stood. "Fine, beer and chess on me. I know just the spot. We'll walk you home first," he added, kissing Sandra's cheek.

"You think I need your protection?"

He gave her a look that told her he didn't care to discuss the matter, and she just smiled and nodded. In truth, she liked when he took on the protective husband role. It suited him, and it wasn't like they were living in some peaceful Nirvana anyway.

"Deal, but you all stumble home. Wake me again, I'm taking scalps." She went to the door and opened it, motioning for Diego to lead the way. He smiled and reached for the door to let her go first, but she stood her ground. If they were going to play protective here, she was going to put her foot down somewhere. She was advancing in her pregnancy, but hell, this pregnant lady had kicked some major ass putting down a mutiny.

"You just keep the bad guys away from my baby," she ordered with a smirk. "I'll open the damn door."

He chuckled on his way past. "Deal."

To her relief they didn't meet with any problems on their walk home, not that the building where they had taken up residence was far. After she had kicked the three guys out of the place she was more than happy to lie down, hands cupping her protruding belly, and close her eyes. Sunset was still a bit away, but she didn't care. This baby inside her was growing and she'd get all the rest she wanted, dammit.

As she drifted off to sleep she imagined a little Diego in there, already practicing his enemy take-downs, and the thought gave her reason to smile.

CHAPTER FOUR

Prince Edward Island

Cammie paced the living room, having just heard Clara's tale about the attempted mutiny by Esmerelda and Presley. She had thought they'd left that city in good hands, but this just served as one more reminder of what she had known all along—Valerie was too trusting.

"All the Golden City Weres were in on this?" Royland asked. He sat opposite Clara and Platea at the table, and was still groggy from having been awakened from his day-sleep.

Clara shook her head. "Some weren't on the inside, but I wasn't close enough to know who. I only started recently."

"After my time, apparently. When I was with the Golden City, all we cared about was survival."

"It could've been your betrayal that led them to this network plan," Royland commented. "I mean, thinking that strong people like you were now against them."

"Thanks," Cammie replied, glaring at him before turning back to Clara. "What can you tell us about it?"

"I honestly didn't know much, but we had a network of communications set up with the Golden City for a bit, or at least we did until it failed. A couple months back, I think it was. Since then, we've only had messages via airship, smuggled aboard for us to find."

"And why would they tell you all of this?" Cammie asked. "It doesn't add up."

"I was on the crew Captain Kaine picked up, and we were the prime source of communications. The plan was to form a network of independents, they called it. Independent communities that would stand up for freedom against... Well, against the likes of you and Valerie."

"Freedom from us?" Cammie chuckled. She couldn't believe what she was hearing. "And you think this is still going on?"

Clara shook her head. "I don't know. I'm not sure how many of the communities were involved in the attack, only that they asked us to be. But either Kaine didn't think it worth his time, or...I don't know, but we didn't go. If others didn't go either, or if Kaine was organizing some sort of coup among the indies after the Golden City Weres moved into Old, er, New York, I wouldn't have known."

"And why not?"

"She left them just before the last mission," Platea interrupted. "It could've meant her life, but you showed up and—"

"And now I'm alive and free," Clara continued. "Thanks to you all, that is. I'd like to request a pardon and be part of this. Whatever this is."

"We're not royalty here," Royland said, dumbfounded. "A pardon?"

"You didn't tell him about your whole captain speech?" Platea asked Cammie.

"It was improvised—a spur of the moment thing." Cammie shrugged at his confused look. "I'll fill you in later."

"And me?" Clara stared up at her with wide, nervous eyes.

"You were part of Kaine's crew and involved in this whole mess, which means you're valuable. And coming to me like this deserves its own reward. There's no need to even ask for a pardon. It's done." Cammie went to them and sat down at the table, taking the fourth seat.

"But?"

"As I said, you can be useful. What else do you know about this network of indies, as you called it?"

Clara glanced awkwardly between Cammie and Royland. "They started as a defense against the creatures of the night."

"Oh yeah, I'd nearly forgotten about the whole hunting us thing," Cammie spat, leaning back. "I'm still waiting to see who comes forward on that."

"They were taken care of," Platea reassured her.

"Focus," Royland added.

"Right." Cammie hesitated. "But I'm not letting that go, not yet. So, you were saying about the indies?"

Clara nodded. "Thing is, we all mostly stuck to ourselves. Supposed to rally if there was a summons, but most of us knew it would never really happen. Now, Toro? They call and we go as fast as our stubby legs can carry us, but not so much with the indies. And that's why I imagine this New York mutiny was put down so fast. It's likely only one or two of the indies around the area responded."

"The rest were too scared of New York, would be my guess," Royland stated. "After what you did to the Golden City, Cam."

Clara's eyes went wide. "Th...that was you?"

With a chuckle, Cammie nodded. "A lot of it, yeah."

"How the fuck am I still alive?"

"Girl, language," Platea snapped, earning a laugh from Royland.

"I still can't get over pirates who care about swearing," he explained.

Cammie stood as she tried to process this information. "We knew there were groups out there, nomad groups and whatnot, but we never imagined that they were working together in some way."

"Valerie will want to know about this," Royland asserted. "It's got to be dealt with."

"For sure." Cammie paused, looking at Clara and her mom. "And someone has to advise New York, and be there so they know who to look out for."

"Hold on there," Platea exclaimed, standing now too. "If you think I'm going to let my daughter leave—"

"No," Cammie interrupted, "I don't. I meant both of you."

For a moment the woman was speechless, then she started to smile. Her eyes roamed to the window as if there were an image of her future there. "Me in New York City, imagine."

"It's not the glamorous city of the gods the legends talk about," Royland commented. "Just…don't say nobody warned you."

Clara was still frowning, however. "You want us to just uproot? Leave?"

"It's smart," Platea told her. "Some of the men might blame you for what happened in the square out there."

"Blame *me?* So I took the guy's knife, that's an invitation to—"

"Not at all," Platea demurred. "But not everyone thinks rationally, especially not pirates. Former pirates. Whatever."

Cammie nodded. "I have a friend here, maybe you know him?"

"We've seen you two and Bronson speaking," Platea told her, "if that's who you're referring to."

"You have a problem with him?"

Platea shook her head and looked at her daughter.

"His kids are nice," she admitted. "I've actually babysat them once or twice."

"Yes, his kids… They don't belong out here with pirates or privateers or whatever you want to call this lot, even if they can hold their own against half the men here. They deserve better."

"And better is New York?" Clara looked doubtful.

"It is. It's not perfect, but they're far ahead of us." Cammie held out her hand, waiting for the girl to shake it. "What'd'ya say? Be our lookout in New York? Bronson will take you there on his airship, and his kids will be safe. The two of you will have a better life, and I believe you'll make the world a better place."

"Damn, Cammie," Royland interjected. "When did you become all gung ho, fighting to save the little people?"

"The day I met Valerie, same as you," she shot back, still waiting with her hand out. "And now, Clara, it's your turn."

Clara bit her lip, eying the hand, then took it in a firm handshake. "It's a deal."

CHAPTER FIVE

The Toro Slums

Circumnavigating the city to make it to the slums undetected took longer than Valerie would have liked, but soon she had them in her sights. Lights from the city were visible in the distance, but the slums were lit only by moonlight and the occasional torch or lantern passing through the night.

Valerie knelt at the edge of a muddy path, rubbing that mud on her pirate jacket and pants. It wasn't like she gave a shit about the clothes. They had been used to go undercover against the Prince, though that hadn't done a lot of good. Now they would be used to go undercover here, in a much less pretty version of undercover.

Martha, on the other hand, was having a hard time.

"Is this really necessary?" she asked, looking at Valerie, Robin, and Rand as they covered themselves in filth.

"You could go back with your nephew," Valerie offered. "The choice is still yours."

"And leave you to have all the fun?" The woman's eyes stared coldly at the slums ahead of them—a wide swath of what could almost be considered houses, if they hadn't been simply cardboard and plywood. With her vampire sight Valerie could make out some of the inhabitants milling about, though they couldn't see her.

"A smaller group could be a good thing," Robin admitted, not afraid to show her feelings on the matter.

"She'll have the best sense of who's who when we get in there," Rand told them, then turned to Martha. "We agreed, that's why we need you. I know my way around there, but when it comes to the pirate council I'm lost."

"All I know is from when three of them visited the Prince, if you call that a visit." Martha smirked. "I wasn't supposed to see the way they treated him, but I can tell you this: these assholes think they're gods."

"Perfect," Valerie exclaimed. "That means they'll be overconfident. Hubris is rarely anyone's friend."

Martha looked doubtful, but didn't say anything further. She knelt beside Rand and started wiping mud on her forehead and sleeves.

"Everyone ready?" Valerie asked, glancing at Robin to see how she was doing.

"Have you ever seen me so dirty?" Robin demanded. Valerie just rolled her eyes.

"I'm not giving you the satisfaction of making some joke about how you're always dirty, or whatever. Plus, compared to Cammie, you're tame."

Robin frowned. "You just don't know me yet. Maybe that's it."

"Or maybe you're teasing me as a way of distracting yourself from what's really going on here." Valerie nodded to the city. "Rand, what's your best guess as to the largest number of slaves. Where they'd be, I mean."

"No guess needed," he replied. "That's going to be in and around the houses of the council. They have slaves catering to them night and day, some on guard even."

"Why don't the slaves just turn on them?" Robin asked.

"Too scared, would be my bet." He turned and lifted his shirt to show his back, where Valerie expected to see whip scars or something. Instead, there were letters on his back. "Every time you offend a non-slave, they play a game with you. The first letter of that person's name gets carved into you. Do it again? The next. When you get the whole name, you change ownership and your life is over, if they so choose."

"You don't have any whole names," Robin noted.

"I'm smart."

"But you still have letters," she pointed out.

"I'm human." After the rest of them had waited long enough, he explained, "I've never met a slave who didn't have *some* letters. You don't get by in there without one of those jerkoffs accusing you of something, even if you didn't do it. They get off on the whole thing."

Robin's hand went to the dagger tucked into the back of her shirt, though there was no one here to attack. The eyes so often hidden behind her gear were visible now since she had removed the mask and hidden it, and they flared red, causing Rand to stumble back.

"If they put even a scratch on my parents, this whole place will fucking burn," Robin stated matter-of-factly. "You can count on that."

Valerie wanted to say something just then, but didn't quite know what. Finally she just nodded and replied, "Damn right."

That had a slight calming effect, due to Robin knowing someone was with her, Valerie guessed.

"Get us there," Robin directed Rand, "now."

The man nodded, pulling his shirt back down, and then motioned them forward. None of them had their swords or other visible weapons since they wanted to go in undetected. Valerie had convinced them that if it really came to a fight, she'd be able to get them weapons. Just take out the first couple attackers, toss the weapons over, and keep moving forward.

As they approached, the mud squished under their feet. The darkness of this part of the city wasn't so different from one particular village she had visited back in France, Valerie remembered. She had walked into the square, pausing to smile at the scent of freshly baked croissants. But when she walked into the bakery, she had been surprised to see a woman bent over the counter with blood pooling beneath her.

The whole place had been torn apart, its inhabitants left for dead.

And for what? All because her brother, under orders of the Duke, had wanted to clear out the area to make way for his warriors and their takeover of the surrounding areas outside of Old Paris.

This wouldn't be the same. This wouldn't be some slaughter, no matter what the people in charge had become.

Emotions rose nearby. Fear, she sensed strongly as they walked past several people. Its strongest broadcaster, however, was right beside her. Robin.

The woman gave her a look that said, "Stay out of my head," and Valerie nodded in apology. She must've betrayed her worry in her eyes. If Robin didn't find her parents, or worse, if she found out they were dead, how would it affect her? Robin was one of the toughest women she knew. How could she not be, having been torn from her parents and forced to become a vampire, then thrown into training to be the ultimate assassin… and surviving?

It didn't matter how strong someone was, though, when their heart was so determined. She could plummet into depression or be driven to a murderous rage. Valerie imagined that, with what the woman was capable of, her rage would end with this whole city in ashes. Robin was still young physically, but mentally she was ready to take on the world. Mentally, she had been through more than most people twice her age. That gave her a maturity, and ferocity, well beyond her years. For the people's sake, Robin's parents had better be unharmed.

The group passed through dark streets that reeked of sewage and tobacco. A wind blew and made the stench worse, the warmth of it seeming like the hot breath of some demon looking down on them from above.

The thought scared her, she had to admit. She was a vampire, and there were more powerful vampires than her out there. There were aliens, even. For all she knew, there could be monsters from other dimensions or spirits. There could be a devil, there could be a god, there could be many gods.

Maybe she *was* a god, in that sense?

She pushed the thought aside and stifled a chuckle, knowing how laughing would look at a moment like this.

It wasn't the right time to get lost in theology or narcissistic musings, she reminded herself. If anything, she wished there *was* a God out there, one being that was controlling everything, to make sure it ended right. One being above it all to ensure that no matter what crazy directions their stories went, at the end everything would end up just as it should. As it was meant to be.

Though she couldn't quite fathom how a god would have let the world sink to this level of fecal existence.

An old man with missing teeth and a cloth over one eye approached her, hand held out as he mumbled to himself. His one good eye stared into the distance as if he didn't really see them, and that's when she realized he was mumbling in French.

"What's he saying?" Martha asked.

She listened for a moment, then shook her head. "You'd rather not know."

"The gist?"

"Stuff he'd like to do to all of us." She walked on, not even acknowledging the man. "It involved replacing his eye with one of ours, and worse. The word for shit was repeated in a fairly incomprehensible way."

"These people," Robin asked, "they're not slaves?"

"Some of them were," Rand replied, "before being cast out of their positions for being too lost…too out of their minds."

"So they wouldn't be much use if we were to ask them questions."

Rand shook his head. "Afraid not. Some people suspect them of faking it, but having lived here I can tell you that a large portion of them really *are* batshit crazy."

"How do they survive?" Robin asked.

"Mostly by begging or looking for scraps, though…"

"Yes?"

"Some still have relatives among the slaves. I think they bring food out here when they can."

"So they steal," Valerie stated. "And I imagine they suffer the consequences if they're caught?"

"Both them and the people they were helping would be executed, yes."

Valerie thought about everything he was saying for a moment as he motioned up a hill to their left.

"I don't imagine there were so many crazy people before the great collapse," she finally stated, keeping her voice down as they passed the torn-out foundations of a house where several of these crazies were milling about, two of them caressing each other in a very disturbing way. "Right? It doesn't meld with all the stories you hear of the glory days of old."

"So what if there weren't?" Martha asked. "Does that change anything now?"

Valerie shrugged. "Might. I don't know. If anything, one has to wonder what's causing it. Are they all really messed up by drugs, as those in New York would have you believe? I'm having my doubts, is all."

"So something has happened that's causing people to lose their minds," Robin cut in. "Sure, it's possible."

Valerie turned to her, sensing a change in her aura. "You've seen something?"

After trudging up that hill in silence and nearly slipping on a muddy patch but being caught by Valerie, Robin nodded. "My gramps. He was still with us for a while. One day he went out to slaughter a chicken for dinner, but didn't come back. Dad went out looking, and when he took too long, I followed. He'd found the old man sitting there with the chickens, staring at the wall of the chicken coop. Just…staring. That look of emptiness never left his eyes, and we couldn't explain it."

"We call that old age, up north," Martha said. "No offense."

"Offense taken," Robin replied with a glare. "It wasn't that. I know the difference."

"And your grandpa?" Rand asked. "What happened to him?"

Robin turned away, continuing up the hill. No answer, but a cold wave emanated from her and Valerie knew to leave it alone. Her best interpretation of that wave was intense sorrow.

They continued in silence past an old building's skeleton, Valerie doing her best to ignore the shapes that could only have been bodies hanging on the front, swinging in the wind.

A deadly silence hung over this area as if even the sounds from the city had been blocked off. Oh, they were still there, but seemed *not* to be at the same time. Lining a nearby street were several stores with large signs in Chinese that had certainly once flashed with the bright lights similar to those in Capital Square in New York; these signs were now broken or hanging sideways. Another storefront had worn-out pictures of nude women, and Valerie had to wonder about the old days again. She had come across a lot of built-up sexual tension among the people of New York, and there were those who had gotten down on the streets at night, including that one bastard she had taken care of later in the bazaar. But stores that dealt in sex? She couldn't imagine what sort of society would condone such a thing.

A yelp came from within, and she had to remember that modern society couldn't be any less harshly judged.

The group paused, glancing at each other, and then Valerie noticed shadows behind them. A small group had gathered and was following them.

"Trouble?" she whispered.

"Only if we don't keep moving."

Again the yelp sounded, this time followed by a man's voice that whimpered, "Please, no more."

"Fuck that," she declared, and turned toward the noise.

She felt for her sword as she approached the door to the place with the sex pics, forgetting that the weapon wasn't there. Her knives would have to do, or she would just go old-style vamp on them—she wasn't sure which.

She pushed through the swinging doors and came to a dark corner, where she took a left and made her way past a curtain into the main area. What she had expected to find was someone getting molested or worse, but what she found instead was a man tied to a cross on a stage and a group of men and women who took turns throwing rocks, pieces of broken cement, and other objects at him.

"Stop, *please*," he begged again, and at that moment the crowd turned to Valerie.

Her companions joined her and Rand mouthed, "Oh, shit."

"We gotta go," he warned, taking a step back. When the others didn't follow, he added, "This is how they do it here. Their justice system, for wrongdoers."

Valerie digested that as she looked at the cuts and welts on the bound man, and she shook her head.

"What has he done wrong?" she asked, addressing the assailants.

"None of your business," a man said, stepping toward her and brandishing a large stick with nails protruding from its top. "Scram, or you join him."

She considered this, then asked Rand, "Does the man likely deserve this?"

Rand's face scrunched up, then he sighed. "I've seen them do this for the wrong reasons."

"Well then," Valerie said, turning back with a wicked smile that showed her vampire teeth and red eyes. "Let's show them what justice really looks like."

"*Le diable*," one of them hissed, stepping back and diving for a machete. Another went for a crossbow, but she held up a hand and *pushed* a slight amount of fear so that they all froze in terror.

"Before you do anything stupid," she stepped forward, letting her fingernails grow into claws, "I want to give you all the chance to leave unharmed. Your masters in this city are about to face justice. You don't have to join them."

When one woman pulled at the arm of a man and he turned and ran off with her, Valerie was glad to see them go. She'd rather not kill anyone she didn't have to. Perhaps this was part of their culture; if they were given fair warning and stopped, she had no problem.

It was the people who knowingly hurt others, especially if they enjoyed it, who she looked forward to bringing to their knees.

So when the rest charged her, she embraced the beast within. But this wasn't about killing them, she decided as the first one swung his nail-tipped stick at her. It was about teaching a lesson, and making a change.

When he came at her again, she decided to have a bit of fun. Instead of tearing him a new one, as her instincts urged her to do, she dodged the weapon, pulled his arm around himself, and slammed the nails through his shirt so that he was pinned to the pillar beside him. The nails had gone all the way in, so he wouldn't be getting free easily.

Then she pulled the rest of his shirt up and over his face, kicked another attacker away, and made three quick scratches across the first man's stomach. The result was a smiley face of blood.

Robin was at her side in an instant, pushing back another attacker with her knife raised when Valerie said, "Wait!"

With a look of confusion, Robin glanced at the smiley face, then frowned. "Don't tell me this place has gotten to you already?"

"In what way?" Valerie asked, turning to toss another attacker onto the stage. She followed in a blur, holding him down with a foot to the throat as she slashed through the bound man's ropes to set him free. She lifted the second man from the stage by his heel and threw him onto the cross, turning as his machete came her way. With a smile, she broke the assailant's wrist, then jammed the machete into the cross at such an angle that it stopped inches from his neck. She did it so fast that neither of them recognized what was happening, and then kicked the original man so that he went flying into one of several booths that lined the room.

"This isn't a game," Robin shouted. "You want to teach them a lesson? Do it with blood!"

Valerie looked at the three she'd dealt with so far while the others backed into the corner, gazing at her in terror.

"No." Valerie took the machete out of the cross, picked up the man and then held him before her, eyes inches from his. "You tell your friends that this is over. The old days are gone, and there *will* be order."

"This isn't what we came for." Rand joined Robin's protest.

Valerie shook her head. "No, but there's a whole city here that needs to change. We can't just let them continue like this."

"What'll you do?" Robin yelled. "Save the whole world?"

With a deep breath, Valerie released the man and said, "Go." He did, along with the others—all but the one still struggling with his shirt. She considered Robin's question, watching the man struggle. When she pulled the stick free to release him, he looked at her with horror and scampered off to join his friends.

"Yes," she stated, turning back to Robin again. "I *will* save the whole world if I can. But I won't be alone. You will help me." She turned to the others. "All of you will. Michael is doing his part, and Akio and Yuko. Terry-Henry Walton, and all the rest of them. *We* will save the whole world, one step at a time."

They heard shouting, then the sound of breaking glass. Fire spread into the room.

Robin gave Valerie an "I told you so" look. "And if it burns before that happens?" Robin joined her on the stage. "What then?"

Valerie shook her head, hoping the ones she had let go weren't behind this. She motioned for Rand and Martha to go out the back door, and then followed with Robin.

"Much of the world might indeed burn," Valerie told her, watching the flames. When they had exited, she saw the group that had followed them and heard them shouting. "Those people and others like them might not make it, or they might change. But in the end, we will win. Out of the ashes, our new civilization will rise."

"You… You're really out there." Robin shook her head. "But we're following you, so it's your call."

Looking between the crowd and the city, barricaded walls not far off now, Valerie made up her mind. "Leave them alone for now. We'll find your parents, then I'll deal with the rest of this mess."

Robin nodded and Valerie felt a surge of warmth from the woman. "Thanks," it said, even if Robin wasn't in a place emotionally to say it out loud.

"This way." Rand gestured for them to follow.

As they ran Valerie was aware of eyes on them, but the people in the shadows neither called out nor attacked. Perhaps they were the ones she had let go, or maybe they were different crazies.

She didn't know how to stop all of this. Hell, she had no idea what needed to be done. But she knew the world couldn't continue on this trajectory, and that if she wasn't the one making a change, nobody would.

It was a heavy weight to carry, but with the powers Michael had bestowed on her she would manage.

CHAPTER SIX

New York

Blue light filtered in through the window, which Sandra took to mean she had woken either in the early hours of the night or late the next morning.

She found a bowl of fruit and took an orange, then made her way to the window and stared out as she ate it. How many other people in this city were staring through their windows at this same moment? It struck her as the thing to do nowadays, since the state of their city and life in general left much room for contemplation.

People were still moving around and the lights were bright in the distance toward Capital Square, so she figured it was night.

The others hadn't returned yet, and were probably tossing a few back as she just sat there being pregnant. At least Diego and Felix could serve as the designated fighters, if it came to it. The fact that they were Weres meant their healing powers would counteract the alcohol before it got too out of hand. And Garcia was a big boy. He could certainly drink his share, but seemed smart enough to know when to slow down.

She took a shower and changed her clothes, thinking she

would go for a quick walk for fresh air. The night sky was clear with no rainclouds in sight; only a few white wisps in the distance.

The hallway's lighting was dim, though at least it wasn't flickering in some horror-story way, but when she reached the elevator she opted to take the stairs instead.

To her surprise, when she opened the door at the bottom of the stairs she found someone there she hadn't expected to see anytime soon. *Jackson.*

"I take it you're looking for me?" she asked.

He stood, hands clasped in front of him, and nodded.

"Val's long gone, if that's what—"

"It's not about her. She had to go, I get it. I've moved on."

"She's not the type you move on from so easily."

He chuckled. "No, she's not. But honestly, I've met someone. This visit isn't about all that though, it's about Loraine."

"The teen you were mentoring?"

"The same."

Sandra stood there waiting for him to go on until finally he said, "Oh, and the baby thing? Congrats!"

"You heard?"

"I keep my ear to the walls, you know."

"The baby thing." She laughed. "Exactly. So how can I help you with Loraine?"

"She's been getting into trouble, and I didn't know who else to go to." He glanced over his shoulder as if someone were watching them, then leaned in. "She's gotten mixed up with the wrong crowd."

"The definition of "wrong crowd" could be a bit murky with you." Sandra wasn't even sure if she was buying this, let alone giving a crap about his problems. Then again, from the little interaction she'd had with Loraine, she knew she liked the girl. With a sigh, she asked, "What kind of crowd are we talking here?"

"Have you heard of the New Wave?"

She frowned and nodded. The name had come up in recent briefings, but she had simply brushed it off as some kids trying to start trouble.

"It's not like the other groups we've had problems with in the past," Jackson went on. "The New Wave believes that Weres and vampires are the next evolution. They practically worship the UnknownWorld, even want to sacrifice themselves for the chance of *evolving*, as they put it."

"Well, shit." Sandra put a hand on her belly, thinking an apology for her unborn having to hear her talk like that—assuming it could hear. "I'm not sure I can help."

"Of course you can. You know Weres and vampires. You're the human with the most inside knowledge. More than anyone *I* know, at least. I mean, you were besties with Val, and now this thing with Diego."

"This thing is a baby," she snapped with a scowl. "And the more you speak, the less I want to help you. But yeah. We should find her, then I can try and talk some sense into her."

"Thank you." He threw his arms around her. "It's not like... I don't know. She's not really my responsibility, but she's kinda become like a little sister."

"Don't worry, we'll figure this out. Hell, we figure everything else out, why not a teenage girl joining a cult?"

He cocked his head. "I'm not sure if that was a joke, but I'm not quite in a jokey mood about this yet."

"Right. Sorry." She gestured for him to lead the way, and followed.

The night had a cool breeze, pleasant and not enough for a coat to be necessary. It rarely was, but sometimes the wind would blow between these buildings and chill you to the bone.

From the corner of her eye Sandra thought she saw someone watching her, but when she looked there was no one there.

Jackson glanced back, worried, but she shook her head. "It

was probably nothing. Any idea where this group could be? This New Wave?"

"Honestly, I hate to admit it, but I followed her once."

"And?"

He looked sheepish as he confessed, "We went toward where I used to tutor her, and then—"

"Lost them?"

He nodded.

"Well, let's start there, then." They started walking, but after a few minutes she paused, heart racing. "How do I know this isn't a trap? It's been a while since I have seen you, then you come out of the blue like this."

"That's the first you thought of it?" he asked. "It should have gone through your mind before you left the building with me so you could've decided on it right away."

"Yeah, well… Call it groggy pregnancy brain."

"If I were trying to hurt you, I wouldn't be doing it like this. I would've just followed you on one of your evening strolls—yes, I've seen you around—and attacked you then. Or taken you somewhere to attack you." He waved his hands at himself, as if to show he was really there. "This is all me right now, no deception."

She pursed her lips, then nodded. "Yeah, and if you tried anything, Diego would snap you in half. So okay."

"Okay?"

"I said okay." She walked forward, leading the way now, but a moment later he caught up.

"What I said was true, about being over Val. But out of curiosity, what happened out there?"

"You mean aside from a bunch of killing and two months of us having no idea where the hell we were going, exactly?"

He nodded. "With Val, emotionally. I sensed something before she left, really. Like we were great together, but there was something distant about her. Ever since that whole 'going into the shadows' moment of her life, I knew it."

"It's hard to think of her as just a woman, just a love interest," Sandra admitted. "Trust me. And for her, too. It's like…life is bigger than all this. Her purpose on this earth is bigger than all this. While we may not understand it, she's here to save the lives of the good and bring justice to those who have committed evil."

"You sound like a weird textbook recounting the story of Valerie the Great."

Sandra laughed. "Maybe that's my job in this world. I'll be the great bard singing the praises of Vampire Princess Valerie."

"I'd pay a few coins to hear that."

"Great, now I have a Plan B for how to make a living if the others decide they don't want my help running the city anymore."

"Hey, if they ever don't want you," Jackson nodded and held out a couple of coins, "we could use someone like you."

"Oh shit, don't tell me you're back at it." She stopped again, but this time more to rest. The baby wasn't that far along yet, but already it was draining her energy to the extent that even a walk like this was tiring. She was glad the whole mutiny thing had happened a week ago and not now. Funny how just a few days made all the difference.

"Back at what?" he asked.

"Factions, all that junk."

"Oh, God, no." He shrugged, looking around. "You all are doing your thing and it's important, I get it. I'm staying out of your way, and we've put our focus more into changing the city in a different way."

"Mind telling me what that is instead of beating around the bush all night?"

He sucked air through his teeth. "Fine, okay? We've started sort of an arts and crafts situation while working to bring help to the homeless. Get their minds functioning well enough for them to get into hotels or at least abandoned buildings instead of staying on the streets."

"You're serious?" She motioned him on, ready to move again. "That's...so not at all what I expected from you."

He laughed. "I could say the same. In fact, a few days ago my mind was in a totally different place. Then I met this woman who was already thinking that way but didn't know how to execute. I have my resources, my people, and she just inspired me. When I say I'm over Val, I promise I have a very good replacement. I'll never forget our time together, but...she fueled the violence in me. Henrietta calms it, makes me a better person."

"You sound like a cheeseball." She laughed. "But you know me, I like cheese. I'm happy for you."

They reached the edge of the square, which was as crowded as ever. It had slowed down for a bit during the violent times, but people were growing bold again, refusing to live their lives in terror.

While cutting through the crowd, Sandra pulled the pregnant card more than once and told people to get the hell out of her way.

When they reached the opposite side not far from her café—which she saw was bustling, thanks to the help she had been able to hire—they made their way over to a side alley beside the building Jackson had indicated.

"Here's the spot," he stated. "This is where I lost them."

She nodded, looking at the brick building and the large trash bins behind them, and then back at the bustling crowds.

A whiff of fresh bread carried to her nose from the café, offset by the smell of trash in the alley. What a weird combination of enticing and retch-making.

Then a thought hit her, and she bent slightly, hoping to kneel, but realizing that wasn't going to happen right now—not in her condition.

"What is it you're looking for?" Jackson asked.

"I remember a story Val told me while we were out there. Before the surprise farewell party, Cammie had taken her to this place underground, through the sewers." She stood, arching her back to stop it from cramping up. "They found Michael's old hideout, she told me, and his old armor."

"And you think this relates...how?"

"She mentioned something about it being around here," Sandra replied. "If this group is all about worshiping his kind and had the slightest idea it was down there, don't you think they'd be doing their best to find his place?"

He shook his head, confused. "But how... Why would they even know?"

"Maybe they were around? Heard us talking?" She racked her brain. "I can't remember if Loraine was at the party, but maybe she heard Cammie and Valerie discussing it there?"

Rubbing his chin in thought, he nodded. "Yeah, okay, I buy it. So we have to go into the sewers?" He gave her stomach a doubtful glance. "Or rather, I do?"

She sighed, glancing in the direction of the building to which Diego might have returned by now, and considered it.

"Forget that, I'm coming," she stated.

"We could wait..."

She shook her head and set about looking for a way in. "Just be ready to grab me if you see me losing my balance or something. I'm sure as hell not going to explain being covered in sewage when I get home."

"Same goes for me." He chuckled and commenced helping her look for the entrance.

She had to do this, she thought to herself. As stupid as it was, she was driven to find this girl and her friends and tell them the truth about what it took to become a vampire or Were.

Although, a small voice from the back of her head said, *maybe they were onto something?* Weres and vampires could heal themselves and move faster, and in many ways were a better version of humans. Well, if you disregarded the problem that most vampires couldn't be out in daylight.

But the fact that most people either died or went crazy during transformation carried a stronger weight in her head, and the one that won out and pushed her to continue and warn these kids.

She hoped they hadn't found a way to try to evolve yet.

CHAPTER SEVEN

Prince Edward Island

Dark waters lapped at the shore, sending spray onto the kids as they played nearby while Bronson prepared the airship. Clara and Platea stood nearby, pulling their jackets tight around themselves to break the night's ocean breeze. While the weather was generally pleasant up here, that wind had a bite.

"You're sure about this?" Royland asked.

"We're now Val's eyes and ears in the northeast," Cammie replied. "Until she tells us otherwise, we hold this place down."

"And if this is all some ploy to make a move on New York?"

Cammie considered the idea, and not for the first time. "I believe Sandra and the rest are capable of dealing with these two if it comes to that."

He nodded. "If it's good for you, it's good for me."

"You know, you're kinda destroying me."

"Impossible."

"Shut up. That right there." She laughed, pushing him away as he tried to give her a kiss. "I'm telling you, I used to be this badass man-eating *chica*, and now what am I?"

"In love?"

"Fuck you."

"What?" He couldn't help but burst into laughter. "I ask if you're in love with me and that's your response?"

"Only because you shouldn't make me have to say it. Don't fish for that kinda bullshit from me."

"Ah…" He nodded slowly, as if she had just let him in on a secret. "So what you're saying is, you have commitment issues and don't like using that horrible, terribly scary 'L word.'"

"Don't psychoanalyze me."

"When you've been alive as long as I have, it's hard not to analyze people to some degree or another."

She just stared at him. Of course she loved him, she supposed. Maybe.

"We're not here to talk about stuff like that," she commented, nodding to Clara and Platea. They were still standing close enough to hear, although both looked like they were trying very hard to pretend they hadn't.

"Right." Royland chuckled, then called to Bronson, "How's she looking, Captain?"

Bronson stood up from whatever he was doing, smiled, and waved them over. "Looks like we're ready. You sure I can't convince you two to come with?"

"We have a duty here," Cammie replied.

He nodded, then noticed a bag of clothes in Platea's hand. "Ma'am, if I may?"

She let him take it from her and smiled as she followed him onto the airship, with Clara close behind.

"This'll be war," Cammie noted. "If it's as bad as that girl says it is, you know it will be."

"And we'll be ready for it," Royland replied. "New York's a fortress, with our Weres and vampires at the ready."

"But Prince Edward Island isn't," she argued. "We have us, but otherwise, what?"

"It's an island!" He laughed. "It'll be easy to keep attackers at bay."

She thought for a moment. "It wasn't so easy when *we* came knocking."

"We knock a good deal harder than most, to be fair."

"And the other pirates out there?" She looked back at the ocean. "Should we go knocking at their doorsteps? We don't know what other horrors await. I say it's stupid to assume we're the scariest monsters around."

"And I say it's foolish to call us monsters." He moved in, putting an arm around her waist. "Well, maybe you're a bit of a succubus, but I'm an angel."

"I'm not about to suck your b…whatever you said, so get your mind out of the gutter."

"No." He laughed. "A succubus."

She removed his hand from her waist and turned to him with folded arms, not sure she liked him calling her names she didn't understand.

With a sigh, he said, "A succubus is a supposedly mythical creature that, as far as I understand the legend, seduces men and then sucks out their soul, or maybe just kills them. Something like that."

"Oh." She considered it, then mustered a seductive grin. "Sure, maybe I am one of those. Sleep tight, and hope you wake up with a soul."

"If vampires have souls to begin with," he replied with a wink.

"You aren't undead, idiot." She hit him playfully, then wrapped her arms around his waist and gave him a kiss. "You heard what Michael told Val about aliens and nanocytes and all that."

He shrugged. "Does that really seem more plausible than ancient curses stemming from Count Dracul or whatever?"

"What're you going on about now?"

He rolled his eyes, but the smile remained. "I keep forgetting that you haven't been around as long as I have, or heard the old stories."

"So some Count was rumored to be the first vampire?"

"Maybe not the first, but definitely the main one. I've heard other stories that some Chinese or Mongolian warlord before him was the real originator, but both of those stories were around the twelve hundred to fourteen hundred A.D. timeframe. I wouldn't be surprised if the Dark Messiah Michael himself created them, or some of his children did. I'd be even less surprised if they were just myths based around the real facts of Michael's exploits. But who knows?"

"I didn't know you were such a scholar." She kissed him again, enjoying this side of him.

"How funny that knowledge of myths is what it takes to be considered a scholar nowadays."

"Hardy har." She turned back and saw that the airship's balloon was filling and the kids were running up the plank to board. "Tell me, what about Werewolves?"

Royland looked up at the sky in thought, likely trying to pull information from some part of his brain he had not used for some time.

"It's all probably as Val told us," he replied ponderously. "But there are other versions. Older tales. I say you should believe what you want to believe."

"I like Val's version, personally. I like the idea that we might get the opportunity to go into space one day and fight evil aliens hell-bent on destroying earth."

"Better than sticking around here wondering which side will win or if we're going to have to face an alien invasion any day soon."

She nodded, lifting a hand to wave to Allan, the Were boy.

Bronson stepped out of the control room and waved too, then cupped his hands and shouted, "Tell Valerie she better come see me sometime. I'm still hurt she didn't say good bye."

"I'll be sure to give her a good punch on the arm for you next time I see her!" Cammie shouted back over the sound of the filling blimp. When it was done, Bronson gave them a final wave and returned to the control room. In a matter of seconds the airship lifted off, given a boost by the antigrav technology at its base.

"You realize that if you punched Valerie in the arm she'd take you down with a flick of her pinky," Royland noted.

"My man has no faith in me," Cammie replied playfully.

"Hey, you've seen her in a fight."

"I'd kick *your* ass at least," she said with a wink.

"This again?"

She had just stepped back and motioned for him to come at her when a shot rang out and they both ducked. A split-second later she'd recovered, eyes searching for the source of the shot.

"There!" Royland shouted, seeing the person first. She spotted more shooters a moment later, but Royland was already moving.

What the hell were they shooting at? Another shot went off and she turned at a *crack* from above. They were shooting at the blimp! That could only mean they knew what Bronson and Clara were up to and meant to stop it.

Not today, assholes.

Cammie darted in the direction of the second shooter, only seeing her in the tall grass because of the glint of moonlight off the glass of a scope. These bastards had a sniper rifle and hadn't told her!

When the woman saw her coming she quickly moved the rifle to fire, but Cammie had already torn off her clothes and transformed into a wolf; she wasn't about to let a sniper rifle get anywhere close to shooting her. She made for the large target fast. With three bounds she was on the woman, teeth sinking into flesh.

Two more leaped out with knives flashing and Cammie spun, growling as blood dripped down her jaw. One sliced from behind and nearly caught her, but she flung herself sideways and then went for his leg.

One bite tore his calf clean off, and as he fell to the ground screaming she moved for the second's throat.

By the time she had turned back to the first, Royland was there, sucking blood from the man's throat.

She transformed back to her human form and, breathing hard, smiled. "You never told me you were into guys. We coulda made that work for us a long time ago."

He pulled back, red glistening on his teeth in the moonlight, and inhaled deep and satisfied. "If it involves an evil bastard who tries to attack the love of my life and me draining his life so I can be rejuvenated, then yes. By that definition, I *am* into guys."

She smirked, then looked up to see the airship moving away. "Think they're okay?"

"They are," he glanced around, "but you need to find your clothes. A group like this can't have their leader streaking whenever she feels like it."

"Shut up." She grinned. "The ocean breeze feels damn good on my exposed skin."

He let his eyes roam and bit his lip.

"Okay, creepo." She started walking back to find her clothes. "Now I'll get dressed. It'll be better for questioning these jackasses, anyway. "She paused, kneeling beside the sniper, and turned her over. To her delight the woman still had life in her eyes, though her breath was coming in quick spurts.

In a flash, Royland had fetched Cammie's clothes and handed them over.

"Thanks," she murmured, wrapping the coat over her shoulders. "Not sure how much time we have here."

"Let's make this easy then." Royland grabbed the woman by the throat, hefting her into the air. "Where're the rest of you? How many?"

The lady stared at him with terror-filled eyes, but clenched her jaw.

"I can end this now, or you can carry your suffering into eternity," he warned her, allowing his fingernails to grow into claws that tore through her skin. "Your choice."

She whimpered and tried to open her mouth, but then just motioned.

"Today's your lucky day," he said, releasing the grip on her neck and taking her by the arm. "Your suffering ends the moment you show us where your compatriots are."

For a moment she looked defiant, until Royland's eyes glowed red and he smiled to show his fangs. She gave a small nod.

"Keep up," he called over his shoulder to Cammie, and the two were off.

"Slow the fuck down!" Cammie shouted as she tied her clothes into her jacket, wrapped it around her neck, and took off bounding after him in her wolf form. She almost wanted to laugh at herself, running through the island like that, jacket probably making her look like a caped superhero.

Super-Were. That would be her name if she ever became a real superhero. Her mind was lingering there and she was starting to think that she really *was* a superhero in a sense when she saw the flash that was Royland and the sniper lady dart across the road.

Following them, she found herself in a two-story house from the old days that had miraculously survived. Men and women were screaming as Royland tore into them, and in a moment Cammie had joined in the fun.

It wasn't that she enjoyed hurting people, or even killing them; it was that she had grown to *love* destroying evil.

And these bastards had tried to kill her friends. As far as she was concerned, there was no greater evil.

Finally, when blood was splattered across the house and all that remained was the sniper lady whimpering in the corner,

Royland darted over to her and snapped her neck, leaving her to crumple to the floor.

"Well, that was exciting," Cammie commented after turning back into her human self.

A gasp came from the stairs and they turned to see a small boy no older than seven staring at her with wide eyes. He didn't look at the blood or the dead bodies; he was just staring at her nudity.

Cammie would have wanted to laugh if it weren't so sad. She shared a look with Royland, one that confirmed he was also wondering what to do about this kid, and then she gave a small, almost imperceptible shake of her head.

Whatever they did next, killing a child would never be considered.

She hoped he hadn't been thinking it, but she had to be sure. While she dressed, Royland approached the boy with his hands out to show he meant no harm, as if that was possible with all the blood on him.

"Are these people your family, boy?" he asked.

The boy finally snapped to attention, though maybe it was because Cammie had her clothes on, and he looked about the room. Tears welled in his eyes, but he shook his head.

"Do you have a family?" Royland asked, now kneeling in front of the kid to block his view of the carnage.

The boy considered this question as if it were difficult, then shook his head again.

Cammie approached slowly and put a hand on Royland's shoulder. "Would you like to come with us? We can protect you."

At this, the boy bit his lip and nodded.

"Come on," Royland offered, holding out his hand. "We won't bite, not you anyway. Only anyone who ever thinks about hurting you."

The boy took the hand, looking at him with total confusion. "I...I don't think that's funny."

Cammie burst into laughter. "The kid's right, dear. Too soon for jokes."

Royland looked annoyed, but he put on a smile. "So the kid talks."

The boy nodded. "I know what you are, and who you are."

"And do you know who you are?"

"Kristof," the boy said. "My parents are on the other side of the ocean. I think. If they're..." His eyes teared up again, but he held it back. "If they're alive."

"You're a strong boy," Cammie told him, taking his shoulder from the other side and helping him walk down the steps.

As they exited the house with him, she saw the look in Royland's eyes and knew he was thinking it too. Now they had more reason to sail than just stopping other pirates. They needed to cross the ocean, to go to Europe.

They would wait for Valerie if they could, but this boy would not remain separated from his parents.

CHAPTER EIGHT

Toro Inner City

Moonlight glinted off the sharp edges of the concertina wire at the top of the wooden planks that kept the crazies of the slums out of the compound of the inner city. Valerie wondered how they would get in without drawing attention.

They made their way along the wall, keeping enough distance that they were able to duck away when they spotted the guard tower nearby.

"Who are these people that they need guards and all this to protect themselves?" Valerie asked.

"Or is it that the people we just pissed off are so dangerous?" Martha wondered quietly, with a glance at Rand. "When the council paid its visit to the Prince, they were hardly guarded at all."

"It wasn't so bad last time I was here," Rand whispered, daring to look around the corner and up at the guard tower. "The guy's even armed. Something happened here."

"You're damn right it did," a voice said from behind them and Valerie cursed herself for not keeping her guard up. When she turned, she noticed that Robin was already facing that direction, hand on her knife. She must've smelled the scent.

With a sniff Valerie confirmed he was just a normal man. When he stepped into the moonlight of the street between them, hidden from the guard tower by the building they were pressed up against, she saw it was the man she had rescued.

"You don't owe us anything." She waved him off. "Go on, before you give us away."

He bowed his head, but didn't move. "The thing that happened here…it was your kind."

"What?"

"Vampires," he replied, eyes glinting. "That's what you are, right? Well, so were they, though less powerful. We fought them off. When I say "we" I mean the guys and gals you went after back there, mostly."

"So why were they attacking you?" Rand asked, leaning forward now.

"I was telling them to prepare, trying to rally them. We fought off the last attack, but I saw them. I saw the vampires, not long ago. A couple walking through the streets, I'd say on a scouting mission, to see what's what before launching another attack."

Robin sneered. "So they tell you you're full of it, but when you insist, they string you up and play piñata?"

"Something like that." His eyes moved to Rand, then paused. "You ain't dead."

"Do I know you?" Rand asked.

"Knew me, kinda. You and my sister."

"Brody?" Rand blushed, then looked around as if he would spot the girl somewhere. "I don't suppose…"

"She ain't been in these parts for some time now," Brody spat, expression darkening. "Not since they took you away and she retaliated for it."

Rand cursed under his breath. "Where? Who?"

Brody pointed at the guard tower. "Top of the top, I hear, but who knows."

"Slave?" Robin asked, and when he nodded, she added, "Looks like we have more of a shared interest than we thought."

Rand just stared at Brody, unable to say another word.

Finally Valerie interrupted the silence. "There isn't a single slave in there we won't set free." She could tell by the look in Rand's eyes that it wasn't only about that, and she got it. Who knows what had happened to her in there. Had they beat her, or worse? Was she still alive? Such questions had to be eating him alive right now, but...

To her surprise, Robin put a hand on Rand's shoulder. She leaned in and whispered, "We'll save her, I promise."

It wasn't that it was uncharacteristic of Robin; she was a caring soul, which was part of what Valerie had found so attractive about her. And she was strong. It was just that in the time leading up to this moment, Robin had seemed so out of it, so distracted and emotional.

Perhaps it was someone else's grief that caused her to pull herself together, but now she stood a little taller, and when she looked at Valerie, there was even a hint of excitement behind those eyes.

"Mind if we stop stalling and get on with it?" Robin asked.

Valerie's eyes went wide, but she nodded and said, "By all means. I could take out the guard, find a way to—"

"No need," Brody said. "Since I snuck out of there, I can sneak you all in."

"And risk your own life?" Rand shook his head. "You can't do that."

"Way I see it is you're about to rescue my sister, maybe take down this whole corrupt city. I aim to help."

"The man knows a way, let him help," Valerie argued. When Rand said no more on the matter, she turned to Brody and smiled. "Welcome to the team."

"Thanks for saving me back there," he replied. "I didn't know where else to go, and I thought that since they'd fended off the attack last time, they could help if I was right."

"Must've been a group of Forsaken that attacked." Valerie glanced at Robin. "This might end up being more than just taking down the city."

She nodded. "If my parents are around, killing local Forsaken won't only be fun, it could be necessary for their safety."

"You don't think they'd want to come back with you?"

Robin frowned and glanced around. "Maybe that's a conversation for another time?"

The tips of Valerie's fingers went numb and her mouth went dry. Was it possible that Robin might not plan on coming back with her? It hadn't even crossed her mind, though she had noticed that since their little make-out session at Slaver's Peak Robin had seemed to be pulling further and further away. At the time Valerie had thought it just meant she was nervous about her parents' safety. She hadn't even considered that it could be something like this, that she might be pulling away because she knew this mission would mean the end of whatever they had going on.

She realized everyone was staring at her and licked her lips to try to get the saliva going again, then nodded.

"Lead the way, Birdy," she directed.

"It's Brody," the guy corrected her with a shrug, "but either way works."

"Sorry." She glanced at Robin, who looked away. "Let's just... get on with it."

Brody sensed that something was up, but after a moment of everyone staring at him he forced a smile. "Your tour begins this way."

He led them away from the guard tower, twisting past buildings to ensure they stayed out of its line of sight, and then started back toward the gate. However, halfway there he paused and smiled, then led them into an old building. It was fairly empty, but had counters and seats along with an old digital board that had been smashed long ago.

"Subway?" Valerie asked, thinking back to the odd system they had developed in New York.

"This was never finished," he replied, motioning to the back room. "Or this part of it, rather. There was a subway in the old days and some of it has been put back into use with a manual push system. But this part? It looks like they were expanding the lines when the collapse happened. Naturally it never was finished and people forgot about it, or most people, anyway."

"If this is here, why haven't the slaves all made a break for it?" Martha asked.

"To face the crazies or slum dwellers?" Rand asked with a scoff. "Lady, half those assholes would sell their own moms if it got them an extra meal."

"That and the danger of the crazies, or worse, creatures of the night?" Brody shook his head. "Not smart. But we didn't even know of the damn vampires—no offense—until they attacked not more than eight months ago. It was like they were staying hidden, trying to keep their secret all this time, and now they just don't care if anyone knows they're out there."

"I still don't see how you lot fought off Forsaken," Robin said doubtfully. "No offense," she added with a hint of a smile.

He chuckled, moving aside a section of the wall that led into a back room. "The people of the slums rose up, but many of them died. People from the inner parts of the city came out with guns blazing, not caring who they hit. Another reason for the fence; the slum dwellers haven't forgiven them for that yet."

"Still… Vampires?"

Brody thought about it a moment, then squinted at Valerie. "To be fair, they were nothing like you. Well, maybe one or two were, here and there. The rest had this more ravenous, almost beast-like feel."

"Ah…" Valerie shared a knowing look with Robin and then

explained to Brody, "Nosferatu. They're a near-mindless version of us. Like if you tried to make a cake and used too much salt, or like the whole thing was just a pile of salt."

Robin laughed at that, and it hurt. That she might not hear that laugh much longer was a thought Valerie couldn't bear, so she returned to the task at hand.

Ahead of them, Brody was leaning over a hole in the ground that he had just revealed.

"We found out about the subway from some old blueprints but couldn't access the main entry point because of a collapse over here. We were able to dig in, though." He started to lower himself down. "This'll get us in there."

"Aren't we lucky we saved you then?" Martha folded her arms and grinned.

"Or maybe it's the other way around," he replied, "since I'd be dead otherwise, and those Nosferatu, as you called them, would likely attack without anyone ready to defend."

Valerie waited while the others entered the tunnel, then followed right behind Robin. She wanted to reach out and take her hand, kiss her, do *something* to ensure she wasn't pulling away, but gritted her teeth and held herself back.

This wasn't about her, not right now. It was about justice, and possibly defending the city against an attack from Nosferatu.

CHAPTER NINE

New York

By the time Sandra and Jackson had found the entrance to the sewers, the noise of people bustling about in the square had died down. She didn't have any idea how late it was, and was starting to think they should just go back to his place and wait there to quiz the girl on her whereabouts when they heard a scream from below.

"I think we're on the right track," Sandra grunted as she lowered herself, reaching out a hand so he could help her the rest of the way.

Just from climbing in there, she was winded. Light filtered in from above in spots where stairs led up, but mostly it was damn dark down here. From what she could see there were a series of metal walkways, just like Valerie had said. The stench wasn't quite as bad as she had been told, at least. Sandra figured that might have had to do with their advanced sense of smell. For once she was glad she wasn't a modified human.

"Hello?" she shouted. "Is anyone down here?"

Sobs sounded in response, then the voice shouted again, "Help!"

"Come on," Jackson yelled, running.

Sandra did her best to keep up but hadn't gone far before she needed to rest. "Dammit!"

This wasn't happening. She was *not* going to get lost in the sewers because she couldn't keep up, so she pushed on.

At a turn, she nearly tripped and was about to curse Jackson's name when he reappeared and grabbed her.

"DAMMIT!" she shouted again, but this time because he had scared her half to death. "Don't you leave me."

He nodded, supporting her as they made their way briskly along the walkways to find the source of the voice.

"Loraine?" he shouted, and a curse followed.

"Leave me alone," Loraine's voice came from the darkness, followed by someone else shouting that they needed help.

"I don't care what drama you're dealing with," another voice said. "Lydia needs our help!"

Finally they saw them, down some metal steps on the edge of a rocky area, almost a cave. One of the girls was on the ground, leg caught in a bear trap. It was bleeding pretty badly, and the girl was unconscious in her friend's arms.

Loraine stood next to them glaring at Jackson and Sandra.

"You followed me?" she demanded.

"We figured it out," Sandra cut in before Jackson had the chance. "What the hell happened?"

"Pretty obvious, lady!" the friend on the ground stated. "Can you get her out?"

"Not likely," came another voice, though it didn't make sense to Sandra how he would be there. She turned to find Diego standing behind them, scowling. He brushed past, darted over to the girl, knelt next to her, and said, "One sec."

Gritting his teeth, he pulled the bear trap apart and shouted for them to pull the girl's leg free.

He took off his outer shirt and wrapped the leg in it, then picked up the girl and said, "Follow me," to the others.

"We... We're not leaving," the friend protested.

Diego just gave her a look, and she nodded and started following him. Loraine was a mixture of furious and relieved, and after a moment she trailed after them too.

"Where're you taking her?" Jackson asked as Diego passed.

"Enforcer HQ to get looked at."

Jackson nodded.

"When I get back, you two can explain what you're doing sneaking around behind my back."

Sandra's mouth dropped. "Excuse me?"

He just kept walking.

"All I did was help find Loraine, Diego," Sandra protested. "Come on."

They all made their way out of the sewers, but now Sandra was too frustrated to think about almost falling or really care about the stench. She kept asking how Diego could lack trust in her, but he refused to talk about it until they had gotten the girl to safety.

"Diego, just listen to me," she demanded as they exited the sewers. With her man's hands full Jackson had to help her again, and Diego didn't fail to notice.

"The wound looks bad," he replied. "I have to get her taken care of immediately."

"Arghhh!" she shouted as he took off into the night.

"I don't mean to sound ungrateful—" Loraine started, but Sandra turned on her, releasing the frustration incited by Diego.

"You! What the hell do you think you were doing crawling around down there? You're lucky you weren't all killed!"

"I...I..."

"You were being stupid, was what you were doing," Sandra finished for her. "And let's get something straight. You couldn't be turned if you wanted to. The chances of dying are just as high as they were down there in that cave. Higher, probably. It's not going to happen, so get it out of your heads right now."

"That's not what we're being told," Loraine countered, and a glance at the friend showed she agreed. "There's a vampire here from up north, somewhere past the Great Lakes, where they're giving the gift to true believers. He says we can go with him when we get enough recruits. We'll be vampires, just like Valerie."

There was too much for Sandra to grasp in those words, so she sat there for a moment trying to understand.

"Wait. Toro?" she finally asked.

"That's…" Loraine shared a surprised look with her friend. "Yeah, but how did you know about it?"

"Holy shitsticks." Sandra lifted her arms above her head, running her fingers through her hair and taking a big breath. "Let me make something clear here. Toro is the city Valerie went to attack. It's not a city full of good guys or good vampires, for that matter. I can tell you what I've seen myself, and that was back in France when a couple of very bad, very powerful vampires tried to make more. Some lived, but the females didn't. They all died. Most of the males turned into mindless zombie vampires known as Nosferatu. Do you understand? Whatever this person promised you, it's all lies."

The girls' faces froze in shock.

"We…we were going to go with them," the other girl whimpered. "We would have been…"

"Fucked." Loraine turned to Jackson, sheepishly. "Pardon my language."

"And the stupidity?"

"Pardon that too?" Her eyes narrowed. "But even if you're right, which sucks by the way, you're not my dad. You shouldn't be all up in my business."

"He probably did help save your life," Sandra argued.

Loraine nodded. "I know."

"I'll tell you what," Jackson offered. "You be smarter, maybe help out with the work we're doing, and I'll back off."

Her friend gave her a shrug and a half-nod and Loraine sighed. "Deal."

"And you, Sandra," Jackson said, turning back to her. "I hope I didn't screw things up too badly by asking for your help."

"I'll send you a bill for the damage," she offered, walking toward Enforcer HQ to check on the girl and find Diego. She left Jackson and the other girls to figure out what was next for them.

It seemed to Sandra like the problems in this city never ended. Whether it was all-out war, mutinous coups, or stopping a girl from running off to join a cult, it just kept going on and on.

CHAPTER TEN

Toro Inner City

The tunnel didn't go far and didn't give Valerie or Robin a problem, since they could see in the dark. Brody seemed to have figured out where he was going with a system where he would keep one hand to the wall, count between gaps, and then reach out again for the wall. It was pretty impressive, especially since there was a drop-off at one point to their left, and they were required to make two turns along the way.

Robin glanced back once, a look of worry creasing her face. Valerie wanted to talk to her, but even a whisper barely audible only to vampires would likely be magnified down here, and the others didn't need to be burdened with their issues. Plus, she doubted she could say anything that would comfort Robin in a situation like this. What did she know of it, after all? Her family were nothing more than fleeting images, bits of memory obscured like darting fish at the bottom of a river.

"Here," Brody whispered, pausing at a staircase.

Robin looked around skeptically. "How is it the council doesn't know about this?"

"Maybe they do," he shrugged, "but they assume it's blocked off, shut down like all the others. What're they going to do?"

"Keep watch at every potential exit point?"

He nodded. "Oh, they do that. We're just going to have to be careful."

Valerie put a hand on his arm. "When we get in there, where would we have the best chance of fitting in?"

He blinked, trying to see her in the dark, but gave up. "You want to fit in?"

"We're here to get my parents," Robin added. "Val's right, we have to stay out of trouble until we know they're safe. Once we have them out of there, we can make a move to free everyone else."

"Damn." Martha scratched her head, frowning. "I thought we were just going to run in there and kill everyone like you did on the island and on Slaver's Peak."

"That's not always the best option," Valerie replied, "as much as these jerks probably deserve it."

Brody sighed. "The munitions factory, though you'll be a cog in the machine, not a lot of room for movement. It's your best bet to go unnoticed, and you might find yourself able to mingle after a couple days, maybe overhear something."

"Good enough," Valerie said, her curiosity peaking. In New York they had weapons and bullets, but most of them had been found on foraging missions or imported via trade with Europe. Back in France she hadn't even considered where the bullets came from. If nothing else, she figured, this trip could be educational.

They followed Brody up, but then he motioned for them to pause. After a moment, he returned with a smile.

"Come on, we got lucky."

Valerie went right after him but then froze, hand reaching for the knife at her waist. The guard was right there, staring at her with his rifle in his hands.

"She don't look so tough," he grumbled, standing aside.

It took Valerie a moment to realize what was happening, but when Brody motioned her onward with a nod of his head she began to get it.

"You bribed him?" she asked.

"Didn't take much," Brody replied. "The guy's kinda with my second cousin, so he's almost family. If we'd gotten the other guard tonight, we'd have to get blood on our hands. Like I said, we were lucky."

"More like the other guard was lucky," she replied.

He chuckled at that. "True enough."

Light fell across the street ahead, the first artificial light aside from lanterns they had seen since entering this city. Valerie heard footsteps approaching and pulled Brody back, the others following her lead.

Two people wearing robes with intricate designs woven into them passed. Valerie considered pouncing, but sniffed and knew more were coming. This second group had more of a smell of sweat and earth to them. Sure enough, moments later a group of soldiers followed, some with blades, others with guns.

Among them were a group of five, two men and three women, wearing tan shirts and pants that flapped loosely around them, chains around their necks as if in decoration.

"The mark of the slave," Brody enlightened them, pulling the others farther into the shadows.

"We're going to have to wear *that*?" Robin asked. "Wait a minute..." She glanced around, listening "Where exactly is this munitions plant?"

Brody pointed to a building not far off. "You're looking at it."

"That's what I was afraid of. If it only operates during the day, well, imagine if they ordered me outside. As a slave, I couldn't refuse. As a vampire, I couldn't comply."

"They wouldn't." Valerie watched the procession turn out of

their sight. "I mean, right? They probably work the slaves to death here, I'd imagine."

Brody pursed his lips in thought. "No, it's a good point. They might not, but you never know with these bastards. They might decide they need her to work elsewhere."

"Does it really make sense for us to all be in one spot anyway?" Robin glanced around the area, thinking. "I mean, there's a lot of ground to cover. What if I make the rounds at night, seeing what I can? Valerie, you do the same during the day, and Rand and Martha can do the munitions factory thing, getting in good with them so they can ask the right questions."

Valerie wanted to argue, if for no other reason than it meant that she and Robin were on opposite schedules. But it made sense.

With a simple nod, she moved on. "Where do we get those outfits, then?"

"Since it's night, it should be easy. There've been a few accidents at the factory, as you would imagine. People's clothes and chains get left behind; the bodies are burned and dumped in the lake."

Robin's face paled.

"No more talk about bodies," Valerie ordered, and then she led the way over to the building. There was a chain on the door, but nothing she couldn't simply pull apart with her enhanced strength.

Brody soon found them outfits and told Martha and Rand where to go the next day, then pointed them to the slaves' sleeping chambers. He explained that it wasn't like there were people watching over them, and with the way the Council sometimes captured new people to be slaves, no one would question two newbies showing up.

"And we're staying with you," Robin stated matter-of-factly.

He turned to her with a raised eyebrow. "If I'm found out, I die, not you."

"They'd have a hard time killing us, that's for sure." Valerie chuckled. "And we'll make sure they have an equally hard time killing you, should it come to that."

He nodded.

"I can't believe I let you talk me into entering Toro and willingly making myself a slave." Martha shook her head and then applied the chain to her neck.

"You think this is bad?" Rand asked with a sigh. "I thought I was free."

"You *are* free," Valerie replied. "Free to walk in here and put that on, and free to take it off whenever you want, really. You can leave right now, as a matter of fact."

He looked to be considering it, then shook his head. "If I did that, I wouldn't be helping all those others taken into slavery."

"You'll do your part then?"

He attached the chain around his neck as his answer.

"Everyone get some rest, if you can," Valerie commanded, glancing at their new outfits and hating that they had to do it this way. It was, however, the best chance of making sure Robin's parents were safe first. "Tomorrow's going to be a big day."

They dropped Martha and Rand off at a shopping mall turned military barracks and continued to a small two-room apartment on top of a closed-down restaurant nearby.

"The sink actually works in here," Brody told them. Then he tilted his head, considering his statement. "I'm not sure if that's as huge a deal everywhere else as it is here."

Valerie smiled. "No, not particularly."

"Ah, well, here you're lucky if you have a working toilet, let alone the sink. Not all do, especially in the slums. They have practically nothing, so you can understand why they're easily upset." He lingered a moment, eyes darting between Valerie and Robin, then smiled knowingly and said, "I'll let you two get some sleep then."

"None for me," Robin replied. She went to the sink, rinsed her hands before splashing water on her face, and then dried them on the dingy hand towel. "I've been waiting a long time to get here. I will sleep when the sun comes up."

"Just…a moment." Valerie turned to see that Brody was closing the door behind him, having entered the other room. She pulled a vial of blood form her coat pocket and handed it to Robin. "In case you come across trouble. I need to rest up if I'm to be out there all day tomorrow."

"Thank you." Robin took the blood and slid it into a pocket of her jacket, then stood there for a moment, staring at Valerie. "You know I appreciate you, right?"

Valerie bobbed her head, but it was a nervous nod. Where was she going with this?

"Everything you've done…" She stepped forward, taking Valerie's hand and holding it to her cheek, then brushing her lips across it in a gentle kiss. "And I know I've been super-distracted."

"With good reason."

Robin nodded, releasing the hand and staring at the floor. "It's like my heart was torn out, gone forever, and now I can hear it beating. Faintly, but it's out there in this city, waiting to be reunited with the rest of me."

She stepped forward so that their bodies were pressed together, leaning her head against Valerie's shoulder, hands gripping her back. This wasn't a hug of comfort; it was more like someone begging not to let her slip away.

"We'll find them," Valerie assured her, and *damn* she hoped that was true. "I'll do everything in my power to find them."

CHAPTER ELEVEN

Prince Edward Island

Cammie woke to find Royland standing beside the bed watching the boy sleep. They had given Kristof the bed while she slept on the couch. Since Royland preferred to sleep during the day, that had been fine, but she hadn't expected him to just stand there like that.

"You creep everyone else out, I get it." She sat up and rubbed her forehead. "Doesn't mean I feel left out, so stop trying so hard to make sure I'm there with them."

He turned to her with a weary smile, then approached and sat down beside her. "Is it creepy that I worry about him? That I want to devote myself to finding his parents, as insignificant as that is in this messed-up world?"

She took his hand, kissed the back of it, and nuzzled against him. "No, that's what makes me love you."

Her eyes popped open. She bit her tongue as she pulled back to look him in the eyes, hoping he hadn't heard her.

FUCK.

He was staring ahead, eyes wide too, and slowly turned to face her. "Ex…excuse me?"

"I said—"

"Nope, there are no take-backs here." He had one leg half-up on the couch. "You said it. Say it again."

"No."

"You can't deny it, Cammie. As much as you want to be the wild one, the cowgirl who thinks she's the Were version of BA, you're just another in a long line of girls in love with me."

"Oh, shut your mouth!" she said, laughing as she hit him.

The boy stirred and she pressed her lips together, pretending to zip them. She'd almost forgotten he was there.

Royland mouthed, "You love me," then jumped out of the way as she tried to kick him. She didn't know why it was so hard to admit…or why it had slipped out.

Dammit, now there'd be no living this down. Now she was… stuck? But it wasn't like she was planning on going anywhere, anyway.

She stood and stomped to the bathroom, pissed at the situation but even more annoyed at herself for being angry at all.

When she stopped in front of the mirror she stared at her reflection and told herself, "Cammie, pull yourself together. You're a grown woman, not some Golden City Were-slut."

She imagined her reflection laughing at her and flashing her breasts before running off to flirt or kill bad guys or whatever the hell normal Weres were supposed to do.

Trying to turn her imagination off, she turned and plopped onto the toilet; not using it, just staring at the wall.

What were they going to do? Here she was acting like a damn teenager while there was a boy out there whose life now depended on her. To make it worse, members of her community had made a move against her and Royland last night, in a way, and there was a major mess to clean up that they had just left there.

Everything was going to change.

No more fucking around.

She stood, then realized she actually had to go to the bathroom. After taking care of business, she stood again, washed her hands, and made for the door.

When she opened it, Royland was standing there, practically beaming.

"Yes, I love you," she repeated, then pulled him in by the shirt and kissed him hard, tongue playing with his. She pulled back. "I fucking love you like I've never loved anything before. So I'll say this once, and only once. I don't care if you're a badass vampire. If you ever hurt me in any way, I will tear out your heart and devour it while you watch. Do you understand?"

He just laughed. "Cammie, I fucking love you too."

She almost pulled him onto the bed at that, but paused when she saw the boy there, still asleep.

"Raincheck?" Royland asked, reading her expression.

"I do have some business to take care of, after all." She turned to the closet and found some clothes.

"What do you have in mind?"

"I'm going to make sure these people figure out who's boss around here. If anyone tries something like that again, they'd better know damn well what their fate will be."

He glanced at the sunlight on the deck and frowned. "It's a shame I can't be there with you. I'd love to see this."

"You would, and it is," she agreed, giving him a peck on the cheek before heading for the shower, "but this can't wait."

"Didn't you shower last night?" he asked, as if an afterthought. "To get that blood off?"

She paused at the doorway. "Sure, but...all that love-talk. You coming?"

"You bet your ass I am." He laughed and pulled his shirt off, revealing his perfect abs.

The morning sun was already hot and humidity was pressing down on the island as Cammie walked toward the house where they had committed their slaughter the night before. On the way, she stopped by the house where William and his crew were staying and told them to follow.

"What the hell happened here?" William asked when they entered the house to see blood still drying on the walls and bodies in all manner of disarray.

"Me," she replied. "Well, to be fair, me and Royland."

"Fuuuuuck," the woman next to William murmured.

"You knew these dicks?" Cammie asked.

The woman nodded. "They used to roll with Bairne, before they tried to betray him once and he cut them loose. Killed their main guy, but let them live."

"Didn't last long," William added. "But I don't doubt they deserved it."

"They did," Cammie replied, then motioned to the bodies. "We're taking them to the square."

The woman frowned. "Not...to be buried?"

Cammie just laughed at that, then motioned to one of William's guys—the tall one. "Run upstairs and grab blankets or towels. Whatever you can find. No use in getting ourselves all bloody if it can be avoided."

He did, and while they waited Cammie walked among the dead looking at their faces. She wasn't sure why, but she wanted to see what sort of expressions they wore in their last moment. It was always different seeing them the next day instead of in the heat of the moment.

"This place...you really think it's capable of change?" William asked, stepping up beside her. The two stared into the face of one of the guys, torn to shreds by Cammie's wolf teeth.

She nodded. "You're here, and I trust you. So far, anyway. If we can continue to build that trust, and you find others *you* can trust... Well, we eventually all trust each other, right?"

"And in the meantime?"

"We use fear." She turned to see the man bringing blankets down. "Which is why we're here today. Can one of your guys find some rope?"

"We're sailors, of course we can get rope."

"Have them bring it to the square." She took one of the blankets and wrapped it around a body, then hefted it over her shoulder. "Bring 'em all."

The group carried the bodies through the streets, earning a number of very curious, very disgusted glances. The blankets didn't cover everything, just enough to keep the carriers clean. Cammie wanted them all to see.

By the time they had reached the square they had quite the following. She estimated that at least eighty percent of the community was there, which would be plenty for her purposes.

Placing the bodies on top of the blankets at her feet so they were on full display, Cammie began pacing, eyes on the dead. William and his crew stood behind her with their hands clasped. Finally she looked up at the crowd, and the low chatter instantly ceased.

This would be enough, she decided. Enough to spread the word to those who weren't here.

"Last night, these people thought to make a move against us," she began, voice raised barely above speaking level. She knew they would listen. "There are two more dead out at the field. I'm here to tell you that this will not be tolerated, that any act of treason against your captain—Valerie—will be punishable by instant death. You should not worry about it in general, because all of you should be happy to live in peace, to thrive in this new system where we do not murder or steal. But let's be clear: you are now under martial law."

She turned, gesturing to William. "These are my right-hand men and women. They will form what nicer communities than this would term a neighborhood watch. The difference here is that instead of reporting you to the police, they *are* the police. Royland and I are the executioners. And believe me, you do not want to meet death the way we would introduce you to her."

"What makes you better than the Prince?" an old man called from the back of the crowd.

"He was fine and dandy with an animalistic society. I…am not. I'm not Valerie, whom you only met briefly. I would love to have the same patience and trust she does, but that's just not the case for me." Cammie stood before them, thumbs in the waistband of her pants, staring down each one in turn. "I am here to ensure your safety, if you're one of the good guys. You want to be a villain," she gestured to the dead, "feel free to join the losing team."

The man seemed okay with that, though some others were exchanging nervous looks.

"Here's how we're doing this." Cammie shouted now, to show how serious she was about all of this. "Each of you will now swear loyalty, but not to me. To each other!"

A few people in the front rows nodded, murmuring in support, which brought a smile to her face.

"We are family now, whether you like it or not," she continued. "Family doesn't turn on each other. Family protects each other, defends each other. Are you with me!"

More cheers now, and even the ones in the back seemed to be getting into it.

"Good," she said as the noise died down. "Because if any of you want to leave right now, you can. You can run west, find another community out there. I promise you, anyone who wants to can leave right now." She paused, letting that sink in. "But if the day comes that we cross paths again and you stand against us, you will die."

Nobody moved. She put her hands behind her back, waiting and watching, almost hoping that at least one person would go.

Then she would know they weren't staying out of fear that she might go against her word and lash out.

She would just have to ensure they all kept their word then.

"Very well," she called to them. "Take a knee, as I will, and repeat after me." They all did, and soon she had them swearing to never turn on each other, to be the family they had never had, and to form a partnership that none could break. They would be brothers and sisters now, led by Royland and herself.

When the rope arrived she had them hang the bodies of the others at the outskirts of town, where most visitors would cross the water. Then, having a bit of fun with it, she used her Were claws to carve a warning sign into a plank of wood.

The sign read, **Pirates, go fuck yourselves**.

When it was over she let her claws retract, brushed her hands on her pants, and paused, looking across the water to the mainland. There, just visible to her because of her Were sight, was a man. He stood in the shadows of a tree, simply staring at them and the island.

"Everything okay?" William asked, coming up beside her.

"We're being watched," she replied, "which could be good or bad."

The man turned and walked away, and soon was gone from sight. She would have to find out who he was, though not necessarily today.

"Set up a couple people to keep watch tonight," she told William, then turned to her followers. "Don't suppose pirates keep any sort of beverage that a bunch of former pirates and I can partake of? Drinks on me!"

A roar of approval rose and they all made their way back to raid the storerooms where the Prince had kept his booze.

"You know," William said as he downed his fourth cup. "You might not be so bad at this leadership thing after all."

"Tell me again when your head's pounding in the morning," she told him, throwing back her drink as well. Of course, she didn't tell anyone it was water; she had made a good show of appearing to drink the alcohol.

They would learn to trust each other. They would learn to be family, but she sure as hell didn't trust them *that* much yet, she thought with a chuckle. She was starting to like them, though. For now, that was enough.

CHAPTER TWELVE

Toro Inner City

Robin wasn't about to sit around wondering what had happened to her parents any longer, not if there was a chance she could find them this very night. The only problem was, she had no idea where to start.

Before heading out she had given descriptions of her parents, as she had last seen them anyway, to the others. She had told them their names, which were Carol and Jack. Nice, friendly names, she had always thought. Simple names, unlike so many she came across nowadays.

With a brief kiss goodnight for Valerie, one that was too distracted to actually mean anything, Robin set off into the night.

She wore the clothes of a Toro slave now. Her plan was to pretend to be on a mission if seen.

Her first step would be to simply get the lay of the land, see if she could find any groups of slaves or others, and ask around. One problem, she began to realize as she made her way to the rooftop and began hopping from one to the next, was that this place was much larger than she'd expected. The area with the dome and surrounding buildings itself was quite wide, and the fence actually extended well past there.

Now that she thought about it, she hadn't visited many big cities. Sure, she had seen New York from a distance, but actually being inside the city was a totally different beast. The thought of it was making her head swim.

When she heard shouting below, she paused. She found a place on the edge of the roof where an old fan or something in a metal box allowed her to lean up against it without being seen in silhouette, if anyone was watching. It was unlikely anyone was, but one could never be too safe.

A group of men and women in old Army fatigues was training, each working on strike techniques as one man led them. It brought back too many bad thoughts of her own training, which had not been so long ago.

She preferred not to watch, so she pulled back and leaned her head against the cold metal, feeling the warm breeze from the lake.

Had it always been this warm so far north? She wasn't even sure what time of year it was anymore. It wasn't like they kept a calendar, though she had seen one once when she was young. Her father had kept it in his garage, where he would try to make old machinery he had found work again.

Her father had never given up. She loved that about him, and imagined it was more about the dream of another time for him than expecting to fix things.

Sadness took over and she just wanted to collapse on the rooftop right there. Having been far away from them for so long she had almost lost hope, which had meant she was able to harden her heart.

But now that she was here and possibly so close to them it felt real, which also meant it felt newly hopeless all over again.

She hated that thought and stood up, walked away from the edge of the roof, and began pacing. Where would her parents be, if they were here? If they had any control over it, that is. They were smart, resourceful… Would they just be putting bullets together like all those others? A cog in the machine? No, she didn't think so.

Her father would *be* the machine. He would show them what he was capable of so that he could find the best possible situation for his wife, even though they were slaves.

That was the kind of man he was.

But what that meant in a place like this, Robin had no idea. She decided that the best way to find out was to get off this roof and start asking questions. And honestly, she thought, doing that as a slave didn't make sense.

Instead of accepting the hand she had been dealt, she moved to the side of the building and started working her way down using a combination of ledges and, when available, fire escapes. Those were broken in some places, completely missing in others.

When she was about twenty feet from the ground she jumped, rolling as she had been trained to do, and came up into the shadows of the building opposite. Here she waited for something to happen with the soldiers, who had moved on to sparring one-on-one now.

To her relief, a moment later one of the soldiers struck his partner too hard, and the partner's response was to put the first in an arm-bar that wrenched his elbow.

After checking him out the trainer sent the first soldier to medical, and that was when Robin made her move.

She slid through the shadows as gracefully as the wind and entered the same building as the soldier, but through a different doorway.

He was hobbling up the stairs in the direction of two voices barely audible through the floor. If she was going to accost him, it would be smart to do so before he reached the top.

Darting forward at vampire speed, she leaped up the stairs, grabbed the man, and pulled him into a chokehold.

"Sorry to do this," she whispered as she felt him stop struggling. He would not be unconscious for long. As she thought about it, this man might have treated her parents poorly. If nothing else, his being part of the city's military helped to keep this system of slavery in place, and he was therefore as much to blame as any of them.

Well, maybe not equally. If she truly believed that, she would have taken his life by now. Instead, she just took his uniform. It wasn't her size, naturally, but she was able to make it work.

Tucking in the shirt at the back and adjusting it so that the creases were under her arms, the bagginess was barely noticeable. It helped that the uniforms didn't exactly fit the soldiers to begin with.

After stowing the man and tying him up so that it would at least take some time before he could raise an alarm, she returned to her original entrance. Once back out in the night she resumed a normal pace, trying to look as if she were on patrol.

As far as she knew looking around while she was on patrol would work for her, so she was able to take it all in for the first time.

Soon she found herself passing the waterfront, where she stopped to gaze at the ocean and watch the moon's reflection dancing in the ripples caused by the wind.

That's when she noticed the warehouse at the other end of the walkway. Its lights were on, and a couple soldiers were milling about in front. She had a feeling about it, so she walked over. To her relief, one of the soldiers was a woman. She wasn't sure why that made her feel better, but it did.

"Hell of a night," Robin offered, stepping up next to her.

The female soldier glanced over and frowned, but nodded.

Robin looked over her shoulder to see light spilling from the building's windows, which were placed too high on the walls to allow anyone to look inside.

"You with Sergeant Krauss?" the woman asked.

Robin nodded as if it wasn't a big deal. "Just making the rounds."

"Sure," the woman said. Her nametag read *Espinoza*, and she wore her dark hair in a ponytail beneath her hat. "That guy's a real prick, eh?"

"I'm not about to badmouth him," Robin replied, but nodded with a "you bet he is" smile. "I'll let you get to it and go back to my rounds. Just, you know…we gotta stick together."

"Sure as hell do." The woman gave her a smile and turned away.

Robin continued past her, thinking this was too easy. A male soldier gave her a nod as she passed and kept moving toward the woman. She found the door to the warehouse and opened it, peeking inside.

Several men and one woman in slave clothes were working on what looked like the base of an air blimp with metal shielding on the bow and a series of openings for rifles or other weapons to fire through.

It was bizarre, to say the least. And fascinating. As she watched, a soldier entered and went to the stern, then climbed into a seat and turned on the airship's leftover antigrav device.

The machine just barely lifted off the ground and two of the slaves took positions behind it. Now she understood. The device would float, with one or more shooters focusing on attack while the others aimed and provided close-combat support if needed.

Toro wasn't just building an army, they were creating a new version of the ancient Roman turtle formation with the help of antigrav technology.

Still, Robin had to chuckle. Against the type of armies that cities had nowadays, they would kick ass. Even used to lay siege to a city the size of New York, maybe, this would be quite useful. But against a couple of vampires? She had her doubts.

As impressive as the attempt was, however, exploring it

wasn't her main goal in coming here. So instead of lingering, she meandered over to the third man in slave clothes.

She stood next to him, watching him fasten metal sheets together, and cleared her throat.

He glanced at her nervously and hung his head, sticking to his job.

"I need you to tell me something," she started.

"Not to disturb, I know the drill," the man replied. "My apologies if I offended."

Robin frowned, not liking how subservient the soldiers had made these people. "I'm looking for a man and woman, slaves just like you."

The man glanced up at her briefly, confusion heavy in his eyes, then returned to his work. "I've not heard of any escaped slaves."

She shook her head. "You've got it wrong. Listen, just...two people, okay? Carol, and Jack. They... Well, they kind of look like me."

He glanced at her again and frowned, then shook his head. "Don't know any by that name, ma'am. My apologies."

Frustration burned, but not because of what he said. It was the look in his eyes. If he *did* know anything, he sure as hell wasn't going to tell her.

She leaned in, about to take a different tack, when a hand landed on her shoulder and caused her to start. When she turned, she found the soldier who had been manning the machine standing there with a frown.

"Corporal, formation outside. Now."

She nodded. "I'll be right there."

"*Now*," he repeated, folding his arms and waiting.

This time she just nodded and turned to follow him out. When this was over, she could come back and question the man again.

But the formation was no formation at all. Rather, it was a

staff sergeant with another sergeant on either side of him, all three of them staring at her with their hands on their pistols. To her relief, the weapons were still holstered. That meant she wouldn't have to kill them yet.

"Let's start with you telling us who the fuck you think you are," the staff sergeant commanded. "Then we can figure out what to do with you."

She hesitated, wondering if maybe she was going to have to kill them after all. She glanced at their chests, glad to see there weren't nametags. If there had been, that would mean she should have one too and lying wouldn't work. Her mind reeled as she tried to come up with something plausible, but it turned out she didn't have to.

"There you are," another staff sergeant called, jogging over to her. "Ramirez, you were supposed to report to me." He turned to the other sergeants and smiled. "Just a mix-up, new recruit and all. You get it."

"Hardly," the first staff sergeant said. He cocked his head at Robin, then licked his lips. "I see you poking around where you don't belong, *Ramirez*, you and I are going to have a problem. The type of problem that ends with my boot so far up your ass you'll have to buy me a new pair. Got it?"

Although she wanted to tear out his throat right then and there, she nodded and turned to follow the new arrival. He led her away from the warehouse and pulled her into the shadows.

"What're you doing?" she asked him.

"I'm pretty sure I'm the one who asks the questions here," he replied, glaring. "If shit-for-brains back there looks into my story, I'll be floating down Shit Creek. So you tell me what you're doing, and I'll give you my answer."

She simply folded her arms and glared.

"You look familiar." He squinted, probably trying to see her better in the darkness. "Do I know you?"

She shook her head. "You wouldn't, no."

"Fine. But here's the deal. The rest of you are over on the other side of town. I thought you lot said you were waiting?"

"My...lot?"

He leaned in, hissing, "The other vampires."

She pulled back, horrified at the thought that he had somehow guessed her secret.

"Oh, come on," he said. "You think I can't recognize you by now? Nobody has skin as pale and smooth as your kind. It's just...unnatural in this world."

"Well, bonus points to you. Maybe I'm just really good at staying in the shade."

He laughed. "Yeah, sure you are. Anyway, you don't have to tell me what you're up to, but try to stay out of the spotlight, okay? I'm putting my neck on the line for this coup as much as any of you."

She nodded, considering the ramifications of what he had just said. There were others like her, vampires, she had to assume, on the other side of town. Brody had mentioned a previous invasion by Nosferatu and some Forsaken, and this had to be connected.

It seemed like some of the inner circle were working with these Forsaken to orchestrate a takeover, and this soldier was in on it.

He started walking away, but she reached out and took his arm. "Wait."

"Yes?"

She wasn't sure what she had intended to say, but simply blurted, "They have me on lookout. Watching this part of town to ensure there are no...surprises. Thing is, I don't have a place to stay yet."

"You... You're asking if you can use my room as a hideout?" He ran a hand through his thick black hair, holding his army cap in the other hand. "Shit, that's risky. I thought they trusted us. This doesn't scream trust."

She shrugged. "It's getting closer and closer, right? Just want to make sure everything's in place."

He frowned. "I'd think two weeks is plenty of time, but if you insist. What can I say to that other than you betcha. Just… When it all goes down, remember your boss's promises."

She nodded, then gestured for him to lead the way.

"I have appearances to keep up, and the job's not done." He took out a keyring and tossed it to her. "Stay out of sight, don't get caught, and if anyone asks, just say we're sleeping together. Better to get hit with fraternization than, well, you know."

A coup to overthrow the council? Yeah, she imagined fraternization carried lesser punishment than that.

"How do I find your place?" she asked.

He gave her directions, then told her not to worry about him, he had another key.

When he had gone, she looked at the key in her hand and smiled. Having two hubs would be useful, especially considering that his was on the other side of town from the room Brody had the others staying in.

Part of her wanted to return there, to check on Valerie and the crew, but she thought this reconnaissance was something she needed to do on her own. They could ask questions at the plant and she would check on them, but to be around them right now, especially Val, was only a distraction.

This man had an in with the military *and* the Forsaken, apparently, and that meant he could be extremely useful. In fact, he had already given her invaluable information. If she wanted to find her parents before the vampire attack came, she only had two weeks.

She would return to the house when she felt like it, but for now, she had to get back to work. She would learn what she could about this place in the meantime, but wouldn't lose focus on the real goal—finding her parents.

CHAPTER THIRTEEN

New York

Sandra was waiting in the lobby when Diego came down looking tired and worried.

"How's the girl?" she asked.

"Not great, but she'll recover." He walked over and sat beside her, taking her hand and kissing her. "There'll be scars, of course."

"She'll have bragging rights."

He smiled.

"Listen, about back there—"

He held up a hand. "No, you were right. You told me it was nothing, and there's no reason for me to think otherwise. Maybe this whole having-a-baby thing doesn't just make the *woman* emotional?"

"Emotional?" She frowned. "Who the hell said I was getting emotional?"

"No, I didn't mean that. I'm just saying—"

"Relax, if you can let *me* off the hook, I can do the same for you." The two stood and nodded to the guards on their way out.

"To let you know, since I don't want you wondering, he just needed help with Loraine."

"And he came to you?"

"I thought that was weird too." She shrugged. "But it all worked out, didn't it? So it must've been the right choice. But get this, the girls were supposed to go with some vampire to Toro, where he promised them they could become vampires."

He turned to her, face losing color. "Can they point this vampire out?"

"It didn't sound like they could, but yeah, that's something we have to explore There might be others that he's roped into this scheme." She shook her head, thinking about this recruiter to the vampire or Nosferatu army out there. "Good news is, if Valerie's up there, the army they're trying to create won't last very long."

"The bad news?"

"That it exists at all, I guess."

They continued walking. When they heard someone laughing, they turned to see Garcia and Felix stumbling back to HQ.

"Hey, there they are!" Felix called.

"Damn, you guys went back for more?" Diego asked. "I figured we closed that place."

"It'll wear off in a few minutes." Felix laughed. "For me, anyway."

"And I'm a big boy," Garcia added.

"A big boy with an important day tomorrow," Sandra noted. "I hope you two aren't jeopardizing this mission. That would pretty much put our safety and our lives at risk."

Garcia seemed to sober up instantly. "Way to kill a buzz, girl."

"My *woman* has a point," Diego barked, then pointed at Felix. "I charge you with taking care of this guy in an appropriate way and getting him lots of water before he goes to bed. Agreed?"

"Yes, *sir*!" Felix gave them a mock salute and the two stumbled off again.

"Wow," Diego exclaimed, shaking his head. "I see why you get annoyed at us now."

She laughed and squeezed his arm. "Trust me, you're much more annoying when you drink."

"Uh, thanks, dear."

They went home and although Sandra still felt quite awake, when she returned from the bathroom Diego had passed out on the bed. She smiled at the peacefulness on his face; such a contrast to the real-world situations they often found themselves in. Pushing his hair back, she kissed him on the forehead and then laid down as well, closing her eyes and trying to ignore her sudden craving for a baguette and cheese.

To Sandra's surprise, Garcia looked as healthy as ever the next day at formation. If he had the slightest hangover, it didn't show. She watched him go through the ranks before sunrise, so that the vampires could be there too. Diego stood at her side, smiling. She knew that as much as he insisted that he just wanted to relax with her, he was itching for more action. She didn't buy his line for a minute.

They had just finished and Garcia had joined them when a voice interrupted them.

"Now there's a face I haven't seen in some time." Sandra turned to see Captain Bronson standing there with three children. He made the introductions.

After a quick hug for each of them, Sandra asked, "What brings you here?"

He stepped aside to reveal a young woman and an older one, mother and daughter by the look of them. "The younger one, actually," he replied. "Her name is Clara."

"It's nice to meet you, Clara," Sandra offered. "How can I help you?"

"Cammie sent me," she commenced telling Sandra all about the network of indies popping up. "They'll eventually make a move on the city. You can count on that."

"Oh, I will!" Diego declared. Sandra had nearly forgotten he was there.

"Clara, this is Diego. And Sergeant Garcia here has been helping to train our army." Sandra waited with a smile as the two shook hands with Clara. "We're partnering with a group based out of the Chicago region. One that is building up a force that, we'd be willing to bet, puts this little group of indie communities to shame."

"When Cammie told me about you all, she didn't mention the hubris," Clara said.

"Clara!" her mother chided. "Sorry about my daughter."

Sandra shook her head. "No worries, truly. She makes a good point. No enemy should be dismissed until they are, well, dismissed."

"Tell her the rest," Bronson advised the girl.

Clara bit her lip. "I think there might be more spies in your midst. Or terrorists, or whatever you want to call them."

She explained the rest of it, and how she knew about Esmerelda and Presley. Sandra nodded, feeling a lump in her throat at the thought of what those two had done and the pain they had caused.

"Too many people died that day," Sandra stated. "None of them had to."

"Well, that's what we're here to prevent."

"No time like the present." Garcia motioned them to the door.

As they walked down the hallway to the elevator, Garcia questioned Clara to find out what more he could. Bronson fell in beside Sandra and gave her protruding belly a curious glance.

"You and…?"

"Diego," she told him with a chuckle.

"The Werecat guy?" He laughed. "I never would have thought

it. You two didn't seem close when you started a war on my ship."

"To be fair, that was caused by pirates, and yeah, when all that was over, he kinda stole my heart."

"Oh, yes, actually I think I sensed something when we next met. I nearly forgot."

"Those were crazy times," she replied. "I was about to say crazier, but I don't know. Harder without Val, for sure."

"Crazier times for me, to be sure." He gestured at the kids behind him. "I try to keep these little ones out of trouble as much as possible."

"Which makes life quite boring," the littlest one noted, earning him a shove from his brother while their older sister rolled her eyes.

Sandra laughed, then had an idea. "Hey, would you kids like to try my famous chocolate croissants?"

"They won *me* over," Garcia called, interrupting his conversation with Clara to impart that apparently vital piece of information.

"And your gut will start betraying that fact if you keep it up," Sandra chided with a smirk. She turned to Bronson and added, "If he hasn't eaten my whole store by now, I'll cook some for the kids."

"They'll love that," he replied.

When they reached the elevator the kids laughed, pushing each other in and then moving up tight to the walls. At a questioning glance from Sandra, Bronson explained that they hadn't had many chances to ride elevators before.

"Damn," she replied. "One forgets about the rest of the world when tied up in here all day."

He nodded with a knowing look. "Give me the freedom of the skies any day, once the pirates are completely gone, anyway."

"Aren't they?"

"Not quite. Most of them over here are gone, but if you cross the water, head over to Europe and then north, they're a force to be reckoned with. They don't call themselves pirates out that way, but it's the same basic idea."

"That so?" Garcia said, his expression going grim. He considered them, then turned to Sandra. "If we have people going back Valerie's way, I might have something worth sharing. A way of communicating with them."

"And you're just telling me this...?"

He nodded. "I only have the two, one for backup. The main one I've been ordered to keep around for comms with Colonel Walton, when needed. But if there's a chance we need to make a move across the ocean, this will come in handy."

"Damn, Sergeant. You're full of surprises."

They kept talking, catching up on the doings of the world, and soon were in the lobby. Clara froze.

"I thought this was going to be pointless," she whispered, then turned to face Sandra. "The one there, over my left shoulder, by the front door."

Sandra glanced over, then back to Garcia. "Know him?"

Garcia scratched his head, trying to make an excuse to look but doing a horrible job. He shook his head.

"I... I should say I'm not positive," Clara corrected herself. "He looks familiar though, and if he looks familiar, I can't imagine why else it would be."

"Do we make a move based on that?" Sandra asked.

Garcia inhaled deeply. "Your call, but I'd say no. Put a tail on him if we can, and make sure we know what he's up to. If he slips up, we make a move. If she's wrong about him, we'll know."

"Get on it," Sandra confirmed, then motioned for Clara and her mother to follow. "I'm going to get a room for you two right by mine. I want guards with you at all times, got it?"

They nodded and the mom said, "Thank you. We... All of this. You don't know how much it means to us."

Sandra hugged her. "I was there once myself. You'll be one of us in no time."

CHAPTER FOURTEEN

Prince Edward Island

No matter how hard she tried, for the whole next day and into the evening Cammie couldn't get that image of the man on the mainland out of her head. The thought of some stranger out there plotting against them, if that's what it was, had an unsettling effect. More than ever, she wanted to get over there and find him and whatever group he belonged to. When she did, she'd be sure to find out what he wanted.

She pushed herself up the stairs to her house, opened the door, and entered to find that Royland and Kristof had setup a game which involved each of them putting apples or oranges in a line, trying to get three before the other cancelled them out with the other fruit.

"You guys made up a game?" she asked, taking a seat at the table.

"He showed me how," Royland replied, blocking a line of two apples with his orange.

"We played it back home," Kristof replied. "Something from the old days. Ticky-toe, I think it's called."

"Ticky-toe?" She leaned back, watching, and couldn't help

smiling at the image of them just relaxing as if this were a world without problems.

"You been up long?" she asked Royland.

He gave her a "you have no idea look" and watched as the boy blocked one of his lines. He paused when he picked up his next orange, then set it back down.

"Well, we know one thing about you, Kristof," he declared. "You cheat."

Kristof laughed, pointing to the two lines he had crafted so that Royland would lose no matter what his next play was. "I set you up, old man. No cheating about it, though. I'm just good at this."

"Better than a…" Cammie turned to Royland with a furrowed brow. "I was going to say a hundred-year-old vampire, but I have no idea how old you really are."

The boy looked away at the word "vampire." He clearly hadn't grown accustomed to it yet, but Cammie hoped that would come in time. Or they would get him back home, one of the two.

"Don't you know it's impolite to ask a vampire his age?" Royland took one of the apples and bit into it, then rolled another to the boy. "Eat up. You gotta keep up your energy."

"You don't know us very well, Kristof," Cammie said, putting on her friendliest smile, "but could you tell us more about where you come from? We'd like to help you get home."

He instantly perked up, though he looked to Royland for a nod of approval before opening his mouth to speak. At least one of them had earned the boy's trust, Cammie thought, trying not to be bothered by the fact that it hadn't been her.

"My father was mayor," Kristof started. "The town is somewhere across the ocean. He was rebuilding it when raiders came. Not these ones, but the old ones. Wearing furry caps with horns and all that. They took me, then sold me to those bad men you killed."

"Can you do your best to remember the name of your town?" Cammie asked.

Kristof leaned back, looking at the ceiling, then shook his head. "Father always said it was good to stay near the center of it all, near the big city but not too close in case there was trouble."

"Near the water?" Royland asked.

The boy nodded, then his face lit up. "The large city nearby… it was called Trondheim, I think. We were close, along a fjord."

"Wait, fjord? And you said furry caps with horns?" Royland considered this with a frown, but then an amused smile crept across his face. "You don't mean Vikings?"

The boy beamed. "That's what they called themselves! Yes! We just called them pirates or raiders, but they insisted they were bringing back the old ways. That they were Vikings."

"Well, shit," Royland said, chuckling. "What has this world come to?"

"Language," Cammie scolded.

He gave her a look that said, "Really? From you?"

"What the hell's a fjord anyway?" she snapped.

"A body of water," he replied. "One of the old Forsaken I used to run with was from that area of the world originally. A land once known as Norway, though he was from another city, one he said had been mostly destroyed during the great collapse. Oslo."

"Could you find the general area?" Cammie asked.

"By myself?" He scoffed. "Not a chance. I was told the general location, or direction, rather, but that's it. However, I'd be willing to bet that at least one of these former pirate captains has had dealings in Europe, or at least knows where we can find someone over there who knows."

The boy looked up at them with wide eyes. "You two…you're serious? You could get me home?"

Cammie smiled. "We're damn sure going to try."

"Honestly," Royland added, "we have no idea what's out there, and we have a duty right now to see this island reformed. But when Valerie returns, yes, we will do our best."

He leaped up and hugged first Royland, and then Cammie. "Thank you, thank you so much!"

"Run along now," Cammie told him, awkwardly returning the hug. "Grab some more food while we chat."

Kristof gave them one more heartbreakingly hopeful smile and took a bread roll and some dried beef into the other room.

When he was gone, Cammie sighed. "Okay, for real now. You think this is possible?"

"If Valerie even lets us go—"

"She doesn't own us."

He frowned. "I didn't mean it that way, but we are all part of something here, aren't we? And you have to admit we're some of her strongest. We have a duty."

"And now we have a duty to him!"

"I'm as onboard with this as you are," Royland hissed. "Don't think otherwise. All I'm saying is, we figure out the best way to go about it without leaving Valerie high and dry."

She nodded, then found some of the dried beef for herself and bit off a chunk. Whoever had seasoned it had done a damn fine job, with just the right amount of pepper and spice. After she swallowed, she said what she imagined they both were thinking.

"Valerie might not even come back this way. She might return to New York in spite of what she said on the subject. And there's that whole going-into-space idea."

"She might have mentioned that." Royland frowned, then shifted uncomfortably. "We'll find out soon enough, I imagine. When has she ever taken her time with anything?"

Cammie nodded. "That's what I thought. I've told William and his crew to get the ships ready, tell the remaining captains that we want to start patrols along our coast, be sure there aren't any pirates coming this way, and spread the word to the trading captains that piracy in these waters is a thing of the past."

"And I'll lead raids inland." Royland nodded his approval. "We'll ensure no indie allies are around and give any nomad groups we find a choice: they join us, or they're against us."

She agreed. "It's the only way to set this place on the right path."

The next day she inspected the ships, both air and sea, out of tradition rather than anything else. Pretty much everyone there knew more about the ships than she did.

She marveled at the way these sailors had managed to refurbish old ships. Even more impressive was the whole airship culture, the idea of which she understood to have been taken from old stories and adapted with the antigrav technology.

They had soon taken to the air, heading inland first while two other captains began scouting missions along the shore.

Cammie hoped to find some sign related to the man she had seen watching them, but that first day they found nothing more than an abandoned shack, the remains of a city from before the great collapse—clearly uninhabitable, as everything had been demolished and picked clean for parts—and miles of deserted, dusty land. She began to tire of all the brown below, to the point that her heart would leap at any sign of green in the distance. Patches of trees grew in spots, mostly gnarled, but some growing tall despite their circumstances.

It wasn't like the old days, from what she understood of them anyway. She had heard stories about this part of the world, the north. Snow and cold and weather like she couldn't imagine. Now it was simply hot all year, with occasional storms.

And this had led to the dead, endlessly dreary scenery she saw before her.

It also led to long moments with nothing to do but chat with

William and the others, and before long she was starting to think of him like a brother.

When they returned in the evening, she gave him a hug and told him to watch his back and be ready to go out on patrol again the next day. Meanwhile, the community on Prince Edward Island was thriving, as she found out when they returned on the third evening.

The sun was already behind the hills to the west when they landed, as they had ventured farther than before, hoping to find something. A gentle breeze came in from the ocean, carrying with it the scent of fish grilled over a fire.

Her belly rumbled and she turned to William. "You better hurry, or there won't be any left after I'm finished."

"Not to worry." Royland appeared on the gangplank of the next closest ship. He was carrying a crate, and three pirates behind him carried another. "Sandra sent a shipment of croissants and a bottle of wine."

"No shit?" Cammie jogged over to help him with the crate and they set it down next to several others she hadn't noticed.

"Our first legally-traded shipment," Royland announced with a smile. "Though I wonder if they told her Val wasn't with us. I mean, she did send one of the nice bottles of wine."

"It's Robin who has a thing for Val, not Sandra."

He shrugged. "They were best friends long before Robin or what's-his-name came along."

"What's-his-name was Jackson, and Sandra and Val were only ever friends." When he gave her a skeptical look, she added, "I have a gift for seeing these things."

"Also, Bronson said thank you," one of the pirates told them, a man she had come to know as Captain Reems. "He and his kids are fitting in nicely, I was assured."

"And the girl?" Cammie asked.

He nodded. "Already doing her part. Heard she outed someone right away."

"Damn. Anyone I'd know?"

"Actually, not a Golden City Were at all." The captain nodded to his men, who headed back to fetch the next crate. "A vampire named Otis. Nobody knew much about him. The type that keeps to the shadows, or...kept. They got the bastard locked up for questioning."

"I'd have killed him."

"They almost did," Reems told them. "Well, Sandra almost did."

"Damn," Cammie nodded approvingly.

"Thank you." Royland gave him a look that told Captain Reems he could and should get back to his duties.

"Oh, just one more thing," the captain said, glancing around. "I don't suppose Valerie has returned?"

Cammie shook her head, ignoring the annoyed look Royland was giving the man.

"Sandra said to pass this on. From a sergeant in New York, said he came over from a certain Colonel Terry-Henry Walton's group." He turned to his personal pack and brought out a small comm device. "Said they want to get it to Valerie ASAP. Solar powered, satellite-operated—whatever the hell that means—and basically should be able to work anywhere."

"No shit?" Cammie took it, staring at the little black device in awe.

"I'd say it's pretty damn valuable, and to be careful with it," Captain Reems said.

"That's likely the understatement of the century," Royland said, now crowding in to have a look too. "Satellites...I've heard that term. Something that man created long ago, an ancient piece of culture that floats in space and once provided communications, entertainment...all sorts of interconnectedness that we could only dream of."

"Until now," Cammie said, beaming. "At least, we have a little chunk of it."

The captain nodded, then turned to go, only stopping at a final "Thank you" from Cammie.

When he was back at the boat, Cammie stowed the comm device and turned to Royland.

"Where's Kristof?"

"The boy crashed early. Kept saying how badly he wants to go on patrol, though. Wouldn't let up on it."

"You know it's too dangerous," she replied.

"Do I?" He laughed. "All I hear is that you sail around being bored."

She frowned, but couldn't argue. "So far," she cautioned, glancing up as the captain and his men carried the last of the crates down.

"How long do we wait?" Royland asked.

"Val hasn't been gone *that* long." Cammie stepped closer, looking into his eyes. "You really care, don't you? I mean, about this boy."

"I really care about getting the boy home so that I don't start caring for him in a way that can't be reality."

"Like a son." She nodded. "I get it."

"I don't think you possibly could," he replied. "Not unless you'd been alive as long as I have. Your mind starts considering everything you've missed out on."

She took his hand and squeezed, not sure what he was saying right now. That he wanted a family? The thought made her want to tuck her tail and run away. Hell, she had only *just* told him she loved him, and she wasn't sure vampires and Weres could reproduce even if they wanted to, especially with each other.

But for now, she held his hand to her chest and told him, "We'll get him home, just…not yet."

"We can't wait forever."

She nodded, considering it, then added, "Maybe I'll take him out next time."

He smiled at that, then took her by the hand to lead her

toward the smell of the cooking fish. "Come on, it's time to fill that belly of yours with the most amazing fish you've ever tried."

"You're speaking my language now, good sir," she replied, happy to follow him and have more positive thoughts to focus on.

When they reached the cookout, the other sailors and community members were already starting to pass around the grilled fish, along with some of the last of the bottles from the Prince's stash.

"I've got a special treat for you tonight," William announced, and everyone cheered.

Cammie perked up when she saw him pull out a strange wooden device with strings on it. When he began to pluck those strings, it was as if she had been pulled away to another time and place. She couldn't remember hearing anything like that.

The sailors loved it and began clapping along, but it was clear William didn't really know what he was doing with it.

"It's called a banjo," Royland whispered into Cammie's ear. "Would you like to hear how it's played?"

"Aren't I already?"

"You're about to." He walked over to William, whispered something in the man's ear that earned him a grin, and took the banjo William handed him.

"Ladies and gents, boys and girls," William shouted, "it appears we have an expert *banjo* player in our midst, as he assures me this thing is called. Well, kind sir, play on." He gave a deep bow to Royland and then stepped back.

As Royland began to play, the world transformed around them. Everyone was into it, clapping, interlocking arms and dancing, and even Cammie found herself spinning and stomping and having a grand time.

On a night like this, she could almost forget about the old days, the times she had been required to take a life so that her own might be spared, or that of a friend. She could forget the pain of those she had seen in the streets of New York, or before that in the nomad tribes and among the crazies out there in the wilderness.

This was life, she thought, as Royland handed the banjo back to William to join her in a dance.

And when he put his hands in her hair and kissed her, she felt as if it were the perfect night. Well, not as perfect as a few minutes later when the two were sitting at the edge of the water, bare feet in the sand, eating grilled fish as they watched the waves.

Now, she thought to herself. *Now it was a perfect night.*

CHAPTER FIFTEEN

Outside New York

The day came for the strike team to make a move on their first target. It was early morning when they set out, but a team of vampires accompanied them in assassin gear taken from the Black Plague to protect them from the sun.

Now that Clara and Platea had filled them in on the situation with the network of indies, it was more important than ever that they take care of the enemy nodes.

And this was no longer a simple strike, it was an intel-gathering mission. Find out who the partners were, and where.

Diego really did want to stay with his wife and unborn child, if for nothing else than to help her around the house. She had shown signs of being exhausted lately, even if she wouldn't admit it, and nausea had woken her up more than she liked to admit.

Still, a part of him looked forward to having an excuse to transform and teach some bastards a lesson. It wasn't that he enjoyed hurting people or killing, when it came to it, but he loved making the world a better place. If it took blood, then so be it.

This wasn't an attitude he liked to discuss openly too often, but it was something he, Garcia, and Felix could all agree on.

"Colonel Walton is going to love this," Garcia noted, running in a crouch to approach the edge of the hill. Diego and Felix were at his side, a small group of Weres and vampires behind them.

A soldier lay in the grass staring forward. He had told them to hang back while he confirmed the location, then motioned to them to advance.

"What're we dealing with?" Felix asked.

"If it were me and my men, I'd say be careful," the soldier told him. "But honestly?" He looked at the Weres and vampires and laughed. "I almost feel sorry for this outpost."

"How many men, soldier?" Garcia demanded. "The last thing we need to do is get cocky and lose someone in battle."

"Right. Sorry, Sergeant. We've been watching this one for almost twenty-four hours, and we're dealing with approximately forty of 'em by my best guess."

"That's nearly two-to-one," Felix said with a smile. "The guy's right. Cakewalk."

Garcia grunted. "Keep the hubris to yourself. Tell the men it's more like eighty, and that they might have some vampires hidden away."

Felix laughed quietly and nodded. "Enjoy the show, Sarge."

"Don't get me started." Garcia pointed a finger at his chest. "Sometimes I think, hey, that guy can heal, what's the big deal if I shoot him in the leg to get him to shut up?"

"Shoot me next time you have the craving," Felix replied. "I like to play rough."

"Okay, boys, enough flirting," Diego interjected. "We have some dickheads to kill."

"That's just the kind of foreplay I need to get ready for this guy." Felix blew Garcia a mocking kiss.

"Hardy har," Garcia replied. "You know that if I ate muffins yours would be the first I'd eat, big guy."

"I don't know what the fuck you two are talking about," Diego said with a chuckle, "but you're making the soldier guy blush."

Not only was the guy blushing, but Diego was pretty sure he was doing his best to not look in Felix's direction. Huh, he'd have to come back to that, maybe hook them up on a date or something.

"Don't forget to leave a couple alive," Garcia reminded them, moving on. "We need that intel."

"Roger that," Felix replied, and turned to Diego. "On your mark."

Diego peeked over the hill to see that it went down into a bit of a decline that led into a field of brown grass and several huts. A guard, if you could call him that, sat snoring on a raised platform with a crossbow at his side.

They'd caught them sleeping. Good.

He was about to give the signal when he noticed something that turned his stomach. Not far from the sleeping guard, in the center of the little community, was a fire pit. Over it was the remains of last night's dinner, and there was no doubt it was a human leg.

"Motherfuckers," Diego spat, blood boiling. "We're keeping *one* alive. No more."

"What'd you see...?" Felix started, but then had a look, too. "Pissant piece of shit."

"Go. Just fucking *go!*" Diego didn't even wait for the others. He was already charging into battle, rifle raised to aim. He paused, brought the guard into his sights, and then *POW!* Brain matter spattered and the guard dropped.

He knew the shot would alert the others, but at this point he really wanted more of a struggle from them. He wanted to see the pain in their faces and the terror in their eyes as they were soundly defeated.

As he'd expected, men came stumbling out of their homes, some pulling on pants, others not bothering; the vampires were moving too fast.

Black forms darted through them like the wind, and they

dropped with thud after thud.

Then a couple up past the main encampment began shooting, and Diego smiled. Good, more of them.

The Weres were transforming now, as more of their team noticed the leg or the skulls Diego now saw piled up next to one hut like a religious offering. The occupant would be the person kept alive for now, he decided.

"Open up," he shouted and kicked in the door, then dove sideways to avoid a shotgun blast. In an instant he was at the man, knocking the shotgun aside and plunging a knife into his upper arm to render it useless.

This dude was large, with a white beard and fierce blue eyes. He wore a vest over his protruding gut and had a long scar across his chest.

When he turned on Diego howling and cursing it must have looked like a straight-up David and Goliath moment, but size had never been a factor for Diego so he just smiled and ducked under the haymaker from the man's other arm. He came up on his other side and landed a knee to the man's groin, but to his surprise, that didn't do much other than piss the guy off.

Fine, Diego thought. *Time to go Werecat on his ass.*

He ducked another strike and transformed into a puma as the man charged him. He was there one moment and gone the next, and the large man went tumbling over his porch's railing to land with a thud on the ground.

And then Diego was on him, growling, teeth tearing into the other arm before he went for the throat.

He stopped himself. This was the one he had wanted alive, so instead of tearing out the man's larynx, he spotted the shotgun he'd swatted aside earlier and dove for it. He snatched up the shotgun as he transformed back into his human form and spun, shoving the barrel directly under the large man's jaw.

"One fucking move," Diego growled. "Please give me a reason."

The man's wild eyes took him in, still fierce at first, but then the fight faded.

"Way to take him down," Felix approached with a smile. "Always better without clothes, I always say."

Diego looked down at his nudity and cursed. "I need to get some stretch clothes that convert with me, like a superhero."

"If you must." He shrugged. He was about to turn back...*KA-BOOM!* A cannon ball ripped right through him, leaving a gaping hole where his stomach had been.

"MOTHERF..." Felix collapsed.

"*Ahhh!*" Diego shouted as he slammed the shotgun into the face of the man below him and then dropped it to drag Felix out of the line of fire. "*GET THE CANNON!*"

Weres and vampires surged up the hill where the shot must have come from and already Diego heard rifles going off. The soldier must've gone around and started an assault on this second, unnoticed base of defense.

Lesson learned, Diego told himself, stashing Felix at the back of a shed. He looked at the hole and cringed, wondering what it would take to heal from that.

He peeked around the building just in time to see a man go flying down the hill, then realized it was only a body. The head came a moment later, followed by cannon debris.

More bodies followed, then all was silent.

"What the hell happened?" Garcia shouted, running forward. He came to a stop next to Felix and started swearing. The soldier they'd been with caught up to them too, then covered his mouth, looking sick.

"Don't you dare say, 'I told you so!'" Diego shouted.

The man stepped back, hands up. "I wouldn't think of it."

"Back off," Garcia ordered. "He's not the enemy here. That man is."

With that, Diego turned back to see the large blood-covered man crawling toward the shotgun.

Diego strode over to him, not even bothering to run. He didn't need to.

He kicked the shotgun away, then stomped on the man's hand.

"Cannibal fuck!" He knelt on the man's throat, preparing to do worse.

"Don't do it," one of the vampires said, hand on his shoulder.

Diego was torn. "That you, Brad?"

The vampire nodded.

"I...I'll talk," the man muttered, his voice choking off at the end.

Diego stood, picked up the shotgun, and aimed it at the man. "You better have something damn good to say." He put the barrel over his shoulder and nodded, feeling a cool breeze on his ass. "I'm going to get dressed. If you're not giving us verbal gold by the time I return, I'm torturing the shit out of you. Literally."

And with that he walked off to find his clothes, almost hoping the man didn't deliver. To his dismay, the man started blabbing almost immediately, going on and on about the different groups nearby, insisting he could show them on a map if they just kept him alive.

Diego sighed, pulling on his pants. It looked like they were about to have another prisoner in New York. But that man had better hope Felix could heal from such an insane wound, or nothing would hold Diego back.

CHAPTER SIXTEEN

New York

The city was peaceful with Diego and the others gone. Not that most people would have noticed, but for Sandra it was a time during which she could finally relax. Peaceful but a bit lonely, she started to think after they had only been gone a few hours. She had to laugh at herself for that.

Getting lazy would be a mistake, she reminded herself, but she knew the vampires had their eyes on the one Clara thought might be a traitor. But until he made a move, they couldn't do anything.

Meanwhile, she had requested that Jackson and the others keep an eye out, and they even had Clara working with them. She figured they would be dealing with a lot of the homeless, the most likely starting point for outsiders if they came into the city. She needed Clara and Platea's eyes and ears at the ready to alert her to anything suspicious. The fact that they both had experience as pirates meant they knew how to fight, which was a plus, but it didn't earn them any trust points even though they had come out with the information before Bronson had a chance to.

She stopped by the café and gave the waitress a nod, then

joined Bronson and his three kids at the bar along the window where they were people watching.

"You all have done wonders for this city," Bronson complimented her. "I mean, compared to when you arrived, this is day to that place's night."

"This city needs to be a place where families can live without worry," she replied. "It needs to be the city people who want peace can come to and maybe buy a slice of cheese and a glass of wine between trips to get new shoes or whatever they choose to do with all that peaceful free time."

"But?"

She sighed. "But we still have a long way to go."

"Even when it's at peace here, you still have the rest of the world to deal with."

"We're working on it." She noticed the youngest boy staring at her, and smiled. "What's your name again?"

"Allan," he reminded her. "You're not one of us?"

"Us?"

He made his eyes turn yellow for a split second, then smiled with sharp teeth.

"Don't do that here, please," she whispered. "And no, but my husband is."

Bronson glanced down at her belly, his expression suddenly serious. "That's right. What'll that mean for the baby?"

"You would know better than I." She laughed. "I mean, you got one out of three, right?"

"Our mom was one," Allan said proudly, "but I was also bitten."

"Interesting," she noted. "So genetics don't make it automatic?"

"Seems that way," Bronson answered. "But I'm hardly an authority on the subject. Just have this little example here."

A Were went running by then, paused, and then turned back

to the window after he saw her. He came in and knelt beside the table to whisper, "He's on the move."

"What? In daylight?"

The wolf shook his head. "Not exactly."

She frowned, then understood. "One of the assassin suits." The vampire Clara had identified must have taken one of the suits Brad and the others had brought with them when they arrived—suits that covered their faces and skin so that the daylight didn't kill them.

"*Merde.*" She stood. "Excuse me. Tell the kitchen I've got you covered."

"You don't have to do that," Bronson argued but she waved him off.

"I want to." She ran outside with the Were and asked, "Which way?"

The Were gestured for her to follow, going back the way he had come and then turning down an alley. "Donnoly was smart, had three pairs of vampires sleeping in the assassin suits so they would be ready in case this happened."

"And they're tracking him?"

He nodded. "One came back to report that they had last seen him at the north side of Capital Square."

She came to a stop and looked back, confused. "So why are we moving south?"

"The Colonel gave specific orders to get you out of there," the Were replied, voice heavy with agitation. "What exactly do you think you'll be able to do that a team of vampires can't?"

She frowned, then said, "To hell with that," and took off running the other direction.

"Don't make me—"

"Make you what?" she called over her shoulder. "I'm pretty sure I outrank you. Try anything, and we'll find out."

She heard him swearing as she turned the corner, keeping to the storefronts as she ran since the majority of the day's crowd was milling about in the square. She would make better time this way.

What the hell did she expect to accomplish? The question repeated itself in her mind over and over as she ran, but she knew she couldn't let that vampire get away. There was clearly a reason for him to be here, and that reason likely had to do with some plot to upset the peace.

That would not be tolerated.

Not in her home, and her home was now New York.

Just past the old billboard to her left, people started screaming and the crowd moved like a school of fish scattering out of the way of an advancing shark.

Two vampires dressed in black went tumbling into the open space they had created and then the moving crowd blocked Sandra's view. Pushing to get closer, she started wheezing for breath but was almost there. The crowd moved again as one of the vampires spun and tore the mask from the other.

Sandra's instincts flared. She had to get everyone's attention before they saw what would happen to that vampire.

"*Gun!*" she screamed, and turned, pointing.

To her relief, more people did the same, acting like a bunch of lemmings and diving out of the way as they screamed and shouted, "Gun!" over and over.

She pushed through them and made it to the circle in time to see the exposed vampire, one she had seen around HQ a few times. His face contorted with pain, and she couldn't bear to watch.

Even as her eyes turned away, she saw the other vampire escaping in a blur of black.

"No," she croaked, trying to catch her breath. Dammit, it couldn't end like this. "*NO!*"

The dead vampire at her feet had his pistol still, so now her gun scare was about to become reality. She dove, unlatched it, and lifted the pistol to aim. Damn, that vampire was fast. He had already reached the buildings and was about to disappear down one of the major streets.

Crack! Her shot made a hole in one of the bricks as the vampire darted out of view.

A moment later there was another *crack,* and the vampire flew back. She stared, confused, until two more black-clad vampires appeared from the same direction. They must've intercepted him.

By the look of their fighting stances these two were well trained, likely from Brad's group.

One pulled a pistol, the other a sword.

Dammit, not here, Sandra thought. "Get him out of the square!" she shouted, running over to them.

The closer vampire noticed her and gave a slight nod, and then the enemy got up and had snatched that one's sword in his moment of distraction. Sandra held her hand over her mouth, pissed at herself for that.

She ran for them, understanding that the situation was better off in their hands but also knowing she couldn't just stand by.

A shot was fired and the enemy vampire stumbled back, then saw a woman fleeing and went for her.

But Sandra was ready. She trailed him, got a good lead, and—

Crack!

Her shot actually hit him! He stumbled forward and sprawled face-first on the cement, sword clattering to the ground.

The two vampires were on him in a second, pulling him back and out of sight. Men, women, and children who had been fleeing moments before started to turn, shouting in confusion, but Sandra stepped out and called, "Enforcer HQ has it under control, ladies and gentlemen," though she wasn't sure any of them could hear her over the noise they were creating.

She ran after the vampires and found them in the shadows, the two having overcome the enemy. They had taken his mask off and stood in the shadows, sword to his throat, pistol to his head.

"Do we need him for questioning?" one of the vampires asked.

"Please say no."

"We can't be executing people—vampires—out in the open streets," she replied, and noted the flash of relief on the enemy vampire's face. She leaned in toward him, holding her pistol at the ready. "Are there others like you?"

He gritted his teeth, refusing to speak.

"You don't want to cooperate?" She smiled. "My boys here would prefer that, right boys?"

"Damn straight," one of them said.

She nodded slowly and repeated her question. "Are there others?"

For a moment the vampire looked like he might answer, but then just closed his eyes as if ready for death.

"Oh, it won't be that easy." She laughed, then turned to the HQ vampires. "Take him around a corner, make sure it'll take him a while to heal from whatever you do, and then get him back to the office for questioning."

She could almost feel their smiles under those masks. The enemy, to his credit, showed no expression of fear. He couldn't hide it in his eyes though.

They went to it, starting with a sword through the enemy's leg to ensure he wouldn't be able to escape. In a flash the three were gone, though she heard the enemy grunting in pain from somewhere not far off.

It was this part of her job that she hated—causing anyone pain, as much as she liked the general idea of the enemy suffering. In her heart she always remembered how easy it was to be unsure which side was right and which was your enemy, so she always felt almost as much pity as sorrow for her enemies. Almost...but not quite.

She made her way back to the square, looking at the crowds gathering, and realized that asshole back there had just set them back two steps in what they were trying to accomplish.

Would the day ever come when the people of New York could

sit back, relax, and know they were safe? She wanted to kick something or take something and smash it.

Instead, she decided to focus that energy on the positive.

She made her way to the building where she knew Jackson had his meetings with the homeless, descended the stairs, and was delighted to find him there with Loraine and the girl from Prince Edward Island, Clara.

They were with a group of shabbily dressed others in a well-lit room. Some decorated pottery, others wove or knitted, many painted.

"You really *have* changed," she said to Jackson.

He looked up from the bluebird he was painting on a plate and smiled. "Sometimes it's necessary."

Sandra just nodded, picked up a paintbrush, and found a spot next to Clara. She picked up a small cup, then dipped a paintbrush in red. Soon she had lost herself in the action of painting tiny red roses just under the edge of the cup. He was right. That little action was like a cleansing bath for her soul. All her worries felt like they were washed away, replaced by a warm pleasantness.

She paused, set the cup and paintbrush down, and put her hands on the small bump of her protruding belly. This was the world she wanted to bring her child into—one that felt like she did right then. Not the one of violence outside. No, that one would be cleaned up well before the baby came, she swore to herself.

"Fartlicking shitbag!" a lady on the other side of the room shouted, causing Sandra to start. She was glad she hadn't been holding the cup or she might have dropped it.

When she looked at Jackson with a frown of confusion, he smiled and just whispered, "It's part of the territory, but the healing process has helped her a great deal. Please, be patient."

Sandra wasn't sure whether to laugh or cry, so she just bit her lip, smiled, and returned to painting her cup.

CHAPTER SEVENTEEN

<u>Toro Inner City</u>

Valerie was growing more frustrated by the day. She stared out through the window, wondering where the hell Robin had gotten to. The woman deserved her space, that was fine and dandy, but leaving them to wonder like this? Not cool.

To make it worse, none of them had found any information on Robin's parents. They had been asking each and every slave they could manage to talk to, but were beginning to draw attention to themselves. No one knew anything, and Martha had reported that the foreman in the factory had taken her aside and warned her people were starting to report her odd behavior.

"The best we can figure it," Rand told them, "the slaves are kept in separate quarters based on the work they do. They wouldn't know each other even if they *were* here."

"Meanwhile we have this council to think of, and who knows what's going on with the Forsaken and their army of Nosferatu." Brody sat in his chair, hands folded in front of him as if he were trying to appear calm. "How much longer do we just wait?"

Valerie knew exactly what they were going through, and they were right. They had waited long enough.

"I'm going after Robin."

They all looked at each other, then turned back to her. "Are you sure?" Martha asked. "All that stuff you said about splitting up, about letting her do what she needed to do…"

"It's clearly not working." Valerie opened the window, glancing at her muddy pirate clothes, and then out into the night. Either way she was going to have to find new clothes, she decided, so wearing clean clothes for now beat those dirty rags.

"And us?" Martha asked.

"There's no need to keep asking if we're not finding anything of value."

"Actually…" Rand held up a finger, hesitant. "I wasn't sure if this was relevant, but there's been some commotion over an event that's coming up. Something that's got them all spooked, but they won't talk about it."

Martha looked at him, nodding. "I'd heard about it. It has them worried."

Considering this, Valerie paused, looking Brody's way. "Is this relevant?"

He frowned, rubbing his hands together. "You might be referring to what the council has been calling the Games. A return to the old ways, they say. Something to inspire and motivate us all—the citizens of Toro. But if it has the slaves worried, perhaps it's something that would affect them all."

"And therefore, it might be where Robin's parents will show up." Valerie had to find Robin before these Games, if for no other reason than to be sure she was aware of them. "Any idea where they will be held?"

Brody laughed. "Where else would games be held?"

Valerie just stared, confused, but Martha answered, "The stadium."

That made sense, but wasn't a welcome answer considering the fact that Robin had been forced to train to be an assassin in an old stadium. Who knew what sort of traumatic memories it might hold for her, or what it would mean going to a large event like this in one.

"Stay out of sight until that day," Valerie commanded. "When it comes, I want you at the stadium, ready to leap at my signal."

"Let me guess, we'll know it when we see it," Rand quipped.

She scoffed. "That's stupid. No, find me, and when all hell breaks loose, I'll signal you with a hand wave or by yelling something like 'kill these rat-bastard fucks!' That'll be the signal."

With a nod, Rand laughed.

"That's my kind of signal," Martha noted.

Not wanting to waste another minute, Valerie went out the window. She turned and looked up the building, seeing no fire escape but plenty of ledges in the darkness. No one would see her climbing up here.

She was fast, leaping to one ledge and holding on, then thrusting herself to the next. Soon she was on the rooftop, and it was just like she was back in New York, looking over the city.

Only now she saw the dilapidated edges of Toro's stadium in a different light. So, they kept it around for a reason. That made sense; it was a large one, after all. But where there had once been a complete dome, she could see it had mostly caved in long ago.

Whatever they had planned, she had a feeling it involved her and the search for Robin's parents.

Knowing this, she had no idea where else to start her search for Robin but over there. She ran along the rooftop and leaped to the next, feeling the rush of excitement in her muscles, the air on her face as she leaped, and then…the building's rooftop gave way under her feet as she landed.

"Oh, shit!" she screamed as she crashed halfway through the old roof, clinging to the edge with her claws so she didn't drop into the darkness below. She pulled herself out and rolled onto her back, just breathing and staring up into the myriad stars.

Damn! She was going to have to remember that this wasn't New York.

With two quick breaths she pushed herself up and moved to the edge of the roof, more cautious this time. Her legs had gotten cut up by the near-fall and her pants were tattered now, but the wounds were healing nicely. That was a definite plus of having Michael's blood in her—healing was much quicker than it used to be.

This time she aimed for the edge of the roof when she jumped, knowing it would provide more support. While it was riskier because she could more easily fall if she misjudged the distance or her trajectory, she wasn't so worried about that.

Most of the night was spent this way, leaping from building to building, then going down to the street, sticking to the shadows and seeing what she could find. It had been fairly quiet, except for a couple of warehouses near the water.

She had gotten close and seen men and women dressed in army fatigues working on military maneuvers. It wasn't exactly out of the ordinary, but after lingering for a moment to try and pick up Robin's scent, she'd decided the woman wasn't nearby.

As the night wore on she found herself caring less and less about sticking to the shadows, and was soon walking along one of the old main streets. It was more polished than the others, and several shops were open.

She paused at one, where an old Chinese man at the counter was painting an oil canvas next to him. It struck her as odd, because his counter had dumplings on it ready to sell while he just sat there painting.

A moment in here wouldn't hurt her search, she supposed. Maybe he would be able to tell her something.

"How much for a dumpling?" she asked. He glanced over, waved her off, and went back to painting.

With a frown, she walked over, set down a coin, and pointed at the dumplings. He eyed her skeptically, assessed the coin, and then simply nodded and handed her a dumpling. She knew that coin was worth at least several or that she should get some change, but the man just went back to painting.

"You speak English?" she asked, irritation rising in her voice.

"Not to slaves who shouldn't have that much money on them to begin with," he replied, not looking at her. "Now get lost and I'll pretend I never saw you."

She leaned over the counter, picked up the bun, and took a bite. The last time she'd had a barbeque pork bun was in a village outside Paris where she'd found a Chinese community. It had been building up as the poor were pushed out of Old Paris, largely to create a safe haven, or so the leadership said. Various ethnic groups had formed communities and some of the best food could be found there, at least until Donovan or his underlings found them and wreaked their havoc.

This bun was twice as good as that one had been, and she found herself wondering what else she had been missing out on in New York.

"You ever thought about exporting these?" she asked.

The man just scoffed.

"You really must be sick of it all, huh?" he asked. "The Games are just around the corner, and you're walking around as if you don't give a rat's ass if you're chosen."

"What would happen then?" She took another bite, blocking him out for a moment as she lost herself in ecstasy.

"Listen, crazy woman. If you don't get the fuck out of my shop—"

She had his shirt bunched up in her hand in a flash of movement, pulling him close. "No, you listen. Just tell me what the hell the Games are and what's going to happen to those chosen, or I'll take you into the backroom and go all Sweeney Todd on you!"

"S…sweeny toad?"

"Just… It's from a story someone told me once. Point is, you die, someone eats you in one of your dumplings or whatever. Now speak."

His eyes went wide as she *pushed* a hint of fear into him. "It's something new the Council is trying…to keep us all scared, I say, though they claim it's some ancient tradition to keep morale up and keep us loyal to them. Hell, if the threat is that we get thrown into a pit to fight for our lives while the rest of the city watches, yeah, I'd say that'd keep us loyal."

Her grip loosened as she took this in. "Fuck…you're saying slaves will be chosen to basically be slaughtered in front of the masses?"

He nodded.

"And if I were looking for two older slaves, say in their late forties, early fifties?"

"You'd better hurry." He pushed her hand away, glaring. "The other rumors say this is a system of age control, to keep the slave population young, healthy, and terrified. Kill off the older ones, so each of those remaining understands that they have to earn their right to live."

Valerie looked down at the delicious pork bun and found that she suddenly didn't have an appetite.

"These Games aren't going to happen," she stated. "At least, not like you expect they will."

He laughed, but when he saw the look in her eyes, his laughter faded. "You're crazy, lady." He glanced at the door, and she could tell he wanted to ask her to leave but was too terrified.

"Don't worry, I'm leaving," she told him, making her way to the door. She stopped there at a box of Chinese sweets, and took them. "I think you owe me at least this much change. Oh, and you can eat the rest of the pork bun, dick."

At least now she knew what was going on, but it was just one more worry to throw on top of the others.

She turned just in time to notice the scent of someone approaching, having been distracted. With a quick side-step she was out of his way, but not before he nearly knocked into her. He paused, glaring at her.

"Watch where you're going," he commanded, then continued down the street.

Except, Valerie caught another whiff from him, one that confused her. It was Robin's scent—faint honey fresh from the comb.

Why the hell did this man have Robin's scent on him?

He glanced back, but she was already in the shadows so she could follow him. When he reached the next street she dashed forward, keeping out of sight. Staying unheard.

If this son of bitch had hurt Robin, he would be found shredded to bits across the city the next morning. Because she needed to know where he was going, she held herself back from doing it right then and there.

They passed a street market where he bought two soups and a side of fried chicken wings, then made for a building opposite, pausing at the entryway to pull out his key.

She watched and noted that the outside door didn't require the key, so there must be a series of apartments inside. When the door had closed behind him, she nonchalantly meandered across the street, ducked inside, and saw him disappear into the first door on her left.

Instead of just bursting in, she listened to the doubt in her mind. Robin had taken off, and this man had bought two soups, and smelled of her.

Valerie suddenly realized with a sickening feeling that she had never really asked Robin about their situation. What were they? Oh, they had passion and a definite connection between them, for sure. But if the woman was here, fooling around with this man, would Valerie be justified in her anger?

She wasn't sure. What she was sure of was that she *had* to know what exactly was going on in there. Instead of waiting or bursting in, she went back out the way she had come in and around to the windows on the side of the building.

It was dark enough that others likely wouldn't notice her and she would be able to see inside without a problem.

To her surprise, there was Robin, accepting one of the soup containers and then sitting down across from the man as if they were old friends.

Valerie rubbed her hand across her mouth, trying to decide what the right move was here.

She sighed, knowing the right move didn't really play a role in this situation because she was who she was. Valerie wasn't the type to just walk away, and she wasn't the type to spy.

No, her way was to go in head-first, so that's what she did.

She marched right back around to the front, pushed through the outside door, stopped at the inside door, and knocked.

When the man opened the door slightly to see who it was, he frowned, glancing at her torn slave clothes.

"I'm guessing this is a friend of yours," he stated, stepping aside to let Robin see Valerie.

Robin nearly spilled her soup as she stood, confusion creasing her brow. "How...what?"

"Did you find them?" Valerie asked. "Because if not, I hope you have a damn good reason for sitting around some strange man's house eating soup with him."

"Wait." Robin stood, eyes going wide. "You don't think...you do! You think the two of us are having a thing here?" She looked at the man and laughed. "Me and him?"

"Hey," the guy protested. "I'm not so bad that it's laughable."

"It's not that," Robin told him, setting her soup down and walking over to Valerie. "It's that I go for a little less meat between the legs."

Valerie frowned as Robin put an arm around her and kissed her cheek, watching as realization dawned on the man's face.

"Ohhh..." His eyes flitted back and forth between them, and then he laughed. "Oh! And...and this is the one you were talking about?"

"You told him about me?" Valerie asked, still annoyed enough to hardly pay any attention to the way Robin's hand was moving lower on her backside. Apparently the woman thought it was funny that Valerie had shown a hint of jealousy, but that's all it had been. A small, insignificant nothing...more of a curiosity than anything else. "How can you possibly think you can trust this man?"

"He's helping, believe it or not," Robin replied. "He put me up here, and has been asking around with his colleagues."

"Really? And did he tell you about the Games and what's going to happen there?"

"I wish I knew," the man said. "See, I've been able to find out there's a coup planned, and..." he glanced at Robin, who nodded for him to continue, "and it involves vampires, or Forsaken as you call them. Something big will happen on the night of the Games, but that's all I know."

Valerie turned to Robin, holding her by the shoulders. "Dear, I think your parents will be thrown into a sort of arena to fight for their lives, along with other aging slaves. It seems we've gotten here just in time."

"Holy shit," the man exclaimed. "Yeah, that...that does gel with everything I've heard, though I hadn't put the pieces together."

A cloud came over Robin's eyes and she looked into the distance. In that moment, Valerie would've been willing to bet that she could've said anything and gotten no reaction.

Finally, Robin turned to them and growled between gritted teeth. "At least we have our mission now."

"We do?" the man asked.

She nodded. "Infiltrate the Gathering, find out what we can about the coup and see what we can do to use that to our advantage. Then we put a stop to the Games."

"I feel like I missed something this time," Valerie interjected. "Gathering?"

The man shifted on his feet, nervously. "There's a celebration held each year to commemorate the time when the Council took control and brought a supposed *peace* to our city, though peace and terror walk a fine line here. All the elite wear the fanciest clothes they have been able to find, old tuxedoes with the holes patched, stuff like that, and they pretend they are the top of society, the pinnacle of man."

"Basically it's an excuse to get drunk and pass out," Robin explained.

"Usually," the man corrected her. "This year it's an excuse to get drunk and hold the Games. I'm guessing the alcohol will serve the purpose of removing the inhibitions of those who can't morally sit by and watch innocents be slaughtered."

"I find the term 'innocent' quite confusing in its meaning nowadays," Robin noted. "But I'll tell you this—my family and others like them fall as close to that line as anyone I know."

"When is this ball, and where do we get our hands on some dresses?" Valerie asked.

The man cringed, glancing between the two of them. "You're sure about this?"

Robin nodded.

"The only place I know of to get dresses would be from the elite themselves."

"Meaning we have to find out where they live and take them."

"And do it on the night of the Gathering while ensuring they are otherwise incapacitated, so they don't go raising alarms."

"Great," Robin said, smiling at Valerie. "Our first big night out together. Should be fun."

Valerie smiled back, taking her hand. "It's all going to work out. You know that, right? I'm going to make sure of it."

Robin considered the comment, then replied, "If anyone can do it, it's you."

"Come on then," the man interjected. "We have some planning to do, and ladies to stalk in order to figure out who you two could pass for."

"Pass for?"

"Yes, lucky for you the Council barely pays attention to the rest of us, but that doesn't mean a couple of outsiders can just go waltzing in there. That is, unless you plan on just killing everyone there."

"No, not yet," Robin replied. "Not like that, anyway."

His eyebrow raised in concern, but he added, "Then let's get to work."

CHAPTER EIGHTEEN

New York

The clouds were yellow with a dark grey lining, signaling the first storm to hit New York since…well, since they had started calling it New York again. Sandra looked up at that sky from the rooftop garden Diego had made for her, trying to force herself not to wonder how he was doing.

Clouds like that wouldn't mean much to a bunch of Weres and vampires, but that didn't help her like the idea of her man being stuck out there in a storm. He was tough, but she had seen his softer sides, the sides that only she knew about.

Like when he would put his head on her belly and sing a lullaby in Spanish. She didn't understand a word of it, but she certainly understood the way his eyes glistened when he was done. Or how he would stare out at the city sometimes, his hand slowly clenching hers tighter and tighter until she had to tell him it hurt. The last time that had happened he'd confessed that he couldn't imagine his child growing up in a city with so many problems, in a world that was so much worse.

"That's why we're trying to make a difference," she had commented.

He'd looked back out at the city, caressing her hand now, fingers pressing into it as if their hands were making love. "No," he told her. "That's why we *will* make a difference."

Damn, she loved that attitude.

He was going to be an amazing father...if he lived long enough for that to be a reality.

At moments like these, all alone in this big city, she let her imagination get the best of her. Her doubts started to rear their ugly heads, and doubts tend to grow when feeding on loneliness and insecurity.

"You up here?" a voice called, and she turned to see the pirate woman Platea.

"Maybe I am," Sandra replied with a smile. "And maybe you should have a seat next to me and enjoy this view before it's ruined by that storm coming in."

Platea nodded and took a seat. She had a kind look to her in spite of the hardness in her face, something sharp in her eyes. With her hair in a bun her features were given more focus and the skin pulled tighter in a way that reminded Sandra of an attack dog. Luckily, this attack dog was on her side.

"You know," Platea began, looking at the city around them, "when I first asked Cammie what treasures she could give us, I had no idea what she meant when she threw New York at me."

"And now?"

"Clara loves it here. I love it here."

"Jackson's treating you two well?" Sandra moved on the bench so she could face the woman. "You know he's had his ups and downs here."

Platea laughed. "So I hear. I also hear he used to date the Vampire Princess herself."

Sandra winced. "I'd think you all wouldn't want to call her that, not after the whole Prince situation up north."

"A corrupt prince doesn't cancel the good deeds of a great princess," Platea replied. "Plus, that guy was self-titled. He came to us as Edward, then started calling himself the Prince. You know, *Prince Edward Island*. Was his name even Edward, though? Half of us doubted it, said he took the name from some old pirate. Edward Teech, and from what I hear our Prince wasn't half the man that pirate was."

"According to some ancient story lost long ago." The thought of what had come before pulled at Sandra's heartstrings, considering how much of it they would never know. She considered the lady whom she would guess was almost twice her age and asked, "What brings you up here?"

"Mostly I just wanted a friend," Platea admitted. "But I'd also heard you were the one responsible for bringing wine to the land, and I have to say, *merci beaucoup*. We found an old wine cellar up north once, back in my nomadic days. It was like heaven until the stuff was gone. I...I wanted to offer my help at the café."

"A former pirate who loves wine?" Sandra laughed. "Sounds like I might be out of business before too long."

Platea smiled and nodded. "I won't deny my love for the liquid bliss, but honestly, I'm cutting back. A glass here and there as a reward for hard work? Some coins to buy a purse? Some new shoes, maybe?"

She held up one of her shoes and Sandra cringed—her boots looked like the backside of a cow that'd been whipped to death.

"How about I start you off with the shoes." She glanced at the clouds, which were slowly rolling into the city. "If we hurry, we can make it and still have time for that glass of wine."

"Oh, but...you can't drink, right?" She glanced at Sandra's belly.

"No, I wouldn't want to risk it with the baby, but people say mixed things on the topic. Doesn't mean I can't enjoy the look of pleasure on your face when *you* have a glass, though."

"Hey, you want to live vicariously through me? I'm your gal."

Sandra made to stand, but Platea beat her to it and held out a hand.

"Thank you." The woman heaved Sandra to her feet. "It's amazing how some days I feel like I could take on the world, but others I'm just beat."

"Welcome to the world of motherhood." Platea wrapped her arm in Sandra's to support her. Sandra didn't need it, but appreciated it nonetheless. In truth, she enjoyed the closeness of another body. She didn't normally feel this needy, but the pregnancy was playing with her emotions and Diego was off to war, or whatever he was up at the moment, and she wasn't herself.

Soon they were at Sandra's favorite shoe vendor, and had just found a pair and paid the man when the raindrops started. Gusts of wind had already started blowing over the shop sign, and the old woman running the place called to her husband to help her put everything away.

"Enjoy the shoes, Miss," the husband offered before locking up and taking off with his wife.

It seemed like everyone was running for cover, knowing how these storms could get. As Sandra led her new friend to the café, she had images of the storm when they had taken down Donovan and his gang. It seemed like ages ago, but it really hadn't been much time at all.

The café was packed. A table in the back was free, but as they made their way to it someone called Platea's name. They turned to see Clara, Loraine, and Jackson.

"This is too weird." Sandra shook her head as she walked over. Not long before Valerie had been dating Jackson, and he had even played a role in the inner circle at HQ. Now he was a random friend they ran into at the café, apparently.

"We can get our own table," Platea told her, having to almost shout above the crowd, who was noisily excited about the storm.

She shook her head. That was Platea's daughter there; how awkward would that be?

So they sat, and Sandra went over and grabbed some wine and

croissants. Apparently they were doing better than usual because a shipment had come in, unaffected by pirates. If this was going to be the way of it going forward, the city could really thrive.

"Hey, aren't you the lady who shot the terrorist?" a man asked, looking at her as she finished setting down the wine.

"Terrorist?" she asked.

"In the square the other day. You know, the one in all black, dressed like the Enforcer Ninjas."

"Enforcer Ninjas?" she looked at the people at her table, perplexed.

"That's what we call your black-garbed fighters. But that one, we saw...yeah, it *was* you! Hey everyone, this is the lady who shot that terrorist guy in the square! If it weren't for you, those two Enforcer Ninjas never would've caught him!"

"Well, I don't know about—"

"Three cheers for... What was your name?"

"That's Sandra," the waitress informed him with a wink. "She owns this place."

"You don't say?" He lifted his wine glass high, and everyone else did the same with their wine, water, or coffee. "Three cheers for Sandra, the hero who takes down terrorists and brings us the best food in all of New York!"

The café erupted in applause and cheers, people toasting her and smiling. It was all a bit overwhelming, so she had a seat, drank some water, and waved a thank you at everyone.

"You are really something." Platea took a sip of her wine. The expression on her face was worth all the embarrassment.

"We're all just trying to survive," Sandra replied.

She took a bite of the potato salad the waitress had brought, then had some more water while listening to Clara tell her mother all about her day helping others. She couldn't help but wonder how this girl had been a pirate only a few days prior.

The back door burst open, causing a bang in the kitchen, and a moment later Diego came rushing in. He was drenched but seemingly all in one piece, much to Sandra's relief.

She bolted up and they met each other, embracing. "What is it? Is everything okay?"

"Felix is in bad shape," Diego answered. "But we took out the first encampment and two more on the way back, thanks to our new source. The whole time I couldn't stop thinking of you. How are you and the baby?"

"Yes, we're good. Great, even."

She beamed, turning to introduce him to her new friends. They wanted to know all about what had happened, but he left out the gory details.

"The main point," he went on, "is that we have what we need. Soon we'll know where all these indies are, where to strike. We're going to send a team to meet up with Terry Henry Walton and the FDG, brief them on what we've learned. I wouldn't be surprised if we have this whole continent squared away before too long."

He reached over and took Sandra's hand, holding it gently, his smile full of all the excitement she felt bubbling inside. But she saw worry there too, worry for his friend Felix.

"We'll go visit him," she leaned in and whispered, "as soon as this storm lets up."

He squeezed her hand. "I'd like that."

"So it's over then?" Clara asked, glancing over at Sandra. "That man they were talking about, he was the one I pointed out?"

Sandra nodded. "You must've seen him when he was traveling around. Seems he was a sort of recruiter for some group up north."

"Wait, what happened?" Diego looked at her, eyes full of worry.

"We found another traitor in our midst, thanks to Clara here." Sandra smiled. "One from Toro."

"Probably good for him we took him down before he got home to find Val doling out justice."

They all laughed.

"It's time to spread the word," Diego banged his fist on the table as if issuing a proclamation, "that those days are behind us. That the indies, the old ways of the Golden City—all of it!—are behind us. We're going to send such a loud message to these jerks who think they can stand against us that their eardrums will explode. And if they still stand against us?" He took a swig of Sandra's water, pausing for effect. "Well, tell 'em Diego's coming."

Sandra cheered at this and the others joined her. The rest of the café, while not knowing what was happening, echoed the cheer regardless, causing Sandra and her companions to burst into joyous laughter, while the rain and winds beat down upon Capital Square just outside.

With windows rattling out there and joy within, Sandra felt at peace. Maybe there really was a chance this world would be a better place by the time her baby came into it.

CHAPTER NINETEEN

Old Canada

Days spent on patrol were starting to grate on Cammie, and she knew it wasn't much better for Royland. Taking the ships out onto the water had its moments, and there was nothing quite like the wind in her hair. Out there the clean air in her lungs was new, fresh. On occasion they would spot old ships and even airplanes downed in the waters, like an ancient burial ground that wasn't so ancient.

What had it been? A little over a hundred and fifty years since all of this had been operational, and now…nothing. Thinking back on it like that, she imagined her great-grandparents or those before them who had lived through that time, a time when people actually sailed through the air in those planes.

Though now that she thought of it, people these days were actually flying in spaceships, if what Michael had told Valerie was accurate.

It made her shudder, the craziness of it all, but also the thought of being up there, being part of it. What other types of technology did they have that she couldn't even fathom? Hell, that her great-grandparents, even in the hay-day of technology during which they had lived, probably couldn't have imagined.

Riding out there on the waves, she had made a decision—if Valerie was going to space, she was going to do her damned best to make sure she and Royland went too.

Then there were days like this where she was on an airship flying over patches of desert and patches of green in the heat, only the cool breeze from being high in the air keeping her sane.

At least she could walk around in the daylight, unlike Royland. And if she got a bit sunburned she would just heal from it, which gave her an advantage over William and the rest.

This was the first day they had taken Kristof with them. None of the land patrols had led to any discoveries or interactions anyway, so she figured it would be good training. Plus, she wanted William to teach him about sailing, both on water and in the air, in case the boy needed something to fall back on. In case they never found his home.

Watching the two of them, she knew Kristof would be a natural. He was young, sure, so he didn't have the strength of the other sailors, but when he was told to pull a rope or hold the course, he made no mistakes.

One of the women relieved a guy at his post, and he came over and sat beside Cammie. His shirt was off, sweat gleaming on his solid dark-skinned chest. When he smiled at her, she noticed he was good looking and found it humorous that she didn't have the slightest bit of attraction toward him.

Damn, Royland really had gotten to her.

"Everything going according to plan?" the man asked.

She nodded, suddenly feeling like the world's biggest jerk for not remembering his name. He had definitely told it to her before, but her mind was drawing a blank.

"It's Derryl," he told her with a chuckle. "The name, I know. Hey, if I'd just waltzed into a new community and suddenly become the leader I'd have a hard time with everyone's names too."

"Thanks, Derryl."

"I mean, I'd probably do *way* better than you at remembering names, but the point is that I get it."

"*Thanks*, Derryl." This time she said it in a tone she hoped conveyed that she wouldn't mind being left alone, but he just laughed.

"Honestly, I'm impressed. William there, he was a tough nut under the old regime. Now you come along, and he sees something in you he always hoped for. Something old Edward always lacked."

"Edward?"

"Shit, girl. You didn't know?" Derryl wiped the sweat from his forehead and held out his hand.

Cammie stared at it, confused, until he nodded to the other side of her where the canteens of water were. She handed him one and said, "Sorry. Know what?"

"The Prince named himself after the island. He thought he was clever, but I thought he was being a douche. Never said that to his face though, or I wouldn't be talking to such a pretty lady right now."

"Watch the flirting, or you won't be doing it for long. Royland gets a tad jealous." She wasn't sure if that was true, but she liked the idea of it being so. "Word gets back to him you were schmoozing me, paying me compliments while half-naked, I don't know…"

Derryl inched away with his free hand up as he took another swig of water. "Don't bite. I'm just being friendly."

Maybe she could buy that.

"What do you want then?"

"Like I said, just playing nice." He handed her the water, but she declined. "If you're as cool as you say you are, I want to know upfront. Call me crazy, but I like to know whose hands I'm putting my life in."

She nodded, liking this guy more now. "To answer your question, it's a bit early to tell, but yes. We haven't had any violence since we made an example of those bastards who were hiding Kristof, and it's probably a good sign that we haven't found anyone on these patrols."

"I'm not following how that's good. Isn't the point to find them?"

She nodded. "But if they've all moved on, maybe because they heard of us, *that* is good."

"Ah."

He looked up then, alert, and she followed his line of sight to William, who had gone to the side of the ship and was shielding his eyes to see better.

"Smoke," Derryl noted, but she had already seen it and was up now too.

"I need two of you to stay on the ship with Kristof," she ordered. "The rest will come with me. Put us down close enough to let them see us, but not be able to shoot at the balloon. We're not going to want to hike out of here."

Kristof turned to her with a scowl, but said nothing. Of course he wanted to go with them, to see the action. That didn't mean he was ready, and no way was Cammie going to put him in jeopardy.

They noticed a group of people as they got closer, more than she would have expected. The smoke carried the scent of burning wood, but no meat. Considering that it was hot and the middle of the day, she knew what was happening before they had disembarked.

Whatever their intentions, these people knew of them and wanted to chat.

Fine, let them say their piece.

Leaving the ship behind, she glanced back and gave Kristof a wave. It was a sign of appreciation for his understanding. He waved back, standing there with his two guards.

From the group of strangers, one man strode forward.

Considering this, she motioned for her group to halt, and then continued to meet the man in the middle ground. She couldn't help but notice how similar this felt to what she had heard the old days of battle were like.

The man came to a stop, and so did she. He was tall, though not particularly muscular. His hair was wavy and he wore a mustache, and there was a pleasant look in his eyes in spite of the scar that ran from his jaw to his mouth, which sort of offset any comfort the eyes gave.

A thought hit her—that man, the one she had seen on the mainland, staring at the island. Now that she thought about it, she was pretty damn sure this was him.

"Why do I have the feeling I've been summoned?" Cammie asked him, nodding to the smoke, then turning to assess the crowd beyond him. More men, not a single woman among them. Interesting.

"I thought about trying a conjuring but didn't really know how, so I figured this was the next best thing." The man's mouth twitched as if he were trying to smile, but then gave up.

"A conjuring? Like… Oh, this is good. Like you think I'm a witch?"

He scowled. "We've heard the stories."

"You've heard them wrong, man." She let her eyes flash yellow and lifted a hand, letting her claws grow. "Werewolf. No dark magic involved, as a matter of fact."

His eyes went wide but the rest of his face refused to show the terror she knew he was feeling. He had likely come into this skeptical that she was anything other than a normal human. Judging by the fact that he had taken her for a witch, he had probably never come across members of the UnknownWorld, Were or vampire.

She kind of wished she had played the role for a bit, but oh well. The wolf was out of the bag now.

"I showed you my dirty secret." She returned to normal so as not to make him piss himself. "Now what's yours?"

He bit his lip, then began, "The locals don't like your presence around here. We were doing just fine before you came along, and we'd be glad to see you go."

"Can't do that," she replied.

"And if we make you?"

She laughed, stopped to see if he was serious, then laughed again. "Listen, little guy. I'm sure you all are tough as nails. I mean, you've got the mustache to prove it. But if a single one of you comes our way carrying a weapon... Well, do I have to spell it out for you? Remember, Werewolf here."

He glanced over his shoulder to where one of his men had stepped forward. In his hand were the leashes of a pack of snarling dogs. One barked at her. Two men nearby revealed crude clubs.

"This isn't a negotiation," the man informed her. "We've come together to deal with this right here. Right now."

She put her hands to her mouth, trying to control her breathing and keep herself from leaping on the guy to tear his heart out. With a deep breath, she remarked, "We have kicked out the pirates. We have made our island peaceful, and now you come at me with threats?"

"I'm telling an outsider that she has one chance to promise she'll be gone by nightfall, or she and her friends die today."

Fury rose up within her, yet she held herself back. "To be clear... I have to ask this. Did you just threaten not only me, but these men and women?"

The man nodded.

"To be extra-clear, I'll tell you there is a small boy aboard my ship. Him too?"

Again the man nodded. "Leave now, or my dogs will tear that boy's face right off."

"You mother-fucking dick-fart piece of lobster shit!" The anger was boiling up; it was too much now. A threat to her was one thing, but to her friends? To that boy?! Hell. No.

When the man pulled a pistol from the holster that had been concealed by his leather jacket, she was all too pleased to attack.

With a sidestep she caught his arm, then moved into him with her forearm raised so that it turned the pistol back onto the man. Before he knew what had happened she had slid her arm along his, taken the pistol, and jammed it into his mouth.

Her leg caught his behind the knee and she pushed him down, twisting him so he faced his own people, gun still in his mouth.

"NOW LISTEN HERE!" she shouted. "This man threatened me and mine, so he will serve as a lesson to you. Surrender, or you all die. Just. Like. Him."

BOOM!

The shot from the pistol rang out, blood and brains splattering across the brown earth, and the man's body fell over.

A moment of silence followed, then a shout rose from the group. Half of them hadn't been sure to begin with, it seemed, since they took off running. The other half came charging right for her, including the man with the dogs.

Dammit, she thought, preparing herself. She hated the idea of hurting dogs.

"What'd you do, Cammie?" William shouted, running up beside her with his rifle at the ready.

"Refused to take shit," she replied, then motioned him back. "Get the others to the ship and hold them off if they make it past me. Protect Kristof."

"You're going to take them all on? By yourself?!"

She nodded and turned back to the approaching crowd, then began to strip. This caught a couple off-guard, but when she dropped her pants and transformed into a large wolf, half of the remaining force broke ranks, screaming as they retreated.

To her pleasure, this included all but the largest of the dogs. She smiled as best a wolf could. That sound of whimpering, them running with their tails between their legs, meant they got to live another day.

There couldn't have been fifteen or so men left at this point, she thought, and charged forward to meet them head-on.

Shots rang out from both sides, one zinging past her and exploding into the ground, another flying just barely over her head. Even if one hit her, she wouldn't care. She'd recover from it…probably.

A man had lumbered over to her, club raised, when a shot from the airship hit him and he fell back. The next was hers and she leaped, taking him down with ease. Blood splattered on her next attacker and he cursed, giving himself away so that Cammie had enough warning to move around him and pull out the bicep muscle on the arm that held his ax.

Leaving him to scream and likely bleed out she transformed, grabbed the ax and the club from the two men, and swung at a group of three. With her Were speed and strength, they were nothing to her.

The next man blinked, clearly not used to seeing a nude woman covered in blood and wielding two weapons coming right for him.

It didn't last long though, since she lodged the ax in his skull before transforming again. Using his collapsing body she leaped for the next, catching his skull in her jaw and twisting, bringing him down so hard that his body twitched twice and went still.

Growling, she spun, eyes piercing the few remaining men.

They ran…all but one.

Instead of giving chase, she transformed and approached, smirking at the line of piss on his green army pants.

His hand opened and the machete he'd been carrying fell to

the ground, followed by the man himself a moment later as he collapsed to his knees.

"Please, please," he begged, staring at her in shock.

"You will tell us where to find the others."

"I will."

"Good." She tried to wipe the enemy blood from her face, but her arms were covered in it too. "Your shirt," she demanded, and when he took it off and threw it to her, she wiped the blood on her face just before it would have dripped into her eyes, then wiped a little smile on her stomach so that her breasts were the eyes. The man just gawked, confused and full of terror.

"Turn that frown...upside down," she commanded, tracing the smile with her finger. She laughed, then cut the laughter off and got in his face. "What're you looking at? Get the fuck up and go deliver yourself to my men so they can debrief you. Hurry your ass!"

His love handles jiggled as he ran and she found herself kinda liking the chubby bastard, even if she had been going to kill him a moment ago. Maybe it was the fact that he was the first shirtless guy she had seen in some time who didn't have perfect abs; not that she disliked a man in shape, but she was starting to feel like everyone around her was perfectly fit, and that was just annoying.

Luckily the shirt was big enough that she could tie it around her midsection, and on the way back she found a corpse with a vest on. She appropriated the vest so that by the time she made it back to her clothes, she wasn't completely nude.

She lifted her clothes and considered them, then realized that if she put them on right away they would be covered in blood and she would be sticky as hell.

"William!" she shouted.

"Yeah?" he leaped down from the ship and started walking over, but froze when he saw her. Several other heads peeked over the side of the ship as if they weren't sure it was okay to look or not.

"God, my bush and nips are covered, okay?" she shouted. "It's not that big a deal."

"Um..." He took another couple steps over, then pointed at her belly with a confused shake of his head. "The...smiley face?"

"I'm fucked up, that's all," she told him, and laughed. "Just, tell Derryl to grab a couple canteens if we can spare 'em. I need to get cleaned up." She glanced around the battlefield and started picking up weapons. "Oh, and tell the sailors over there that, no, they cannot watch."

"Yes, ma'am." He ran back to relay the message.

Soon she had a couple of cool new axes and a club in her arms and two old-looking rifles slung over her shoulders. She made it to the ship, where Derryl had thoughtfully left the canteens.

She unloaded the weapons, glancing around to see that her orders had been followed—not that she gave a damn, but figured Royland wouldn't like it if she knowingly let a group of guys watch her bathe—and then got down to scrubbing the blood off. At least most of it hadn't dried yet. Dried blood stained the skin if left for too long; she had learned that from experience.

The vest worked well as a washcloth, and when she was done she dressed in her old clothes. She had gathered up her loot and was going to board when she heard growling from the other side of the airship.

Great, she thought. *More of those damn dogs.*

Then her heart froze at the sound of Kristof's voice. Her legs moved on instinct, claws extending from her fingertips, and she rounded the ship to find the boy there, rubbing the ears of one of the dogs.

It growled playfully, then rolled over for him to rub its belly.

She just stared for a moment, horrified by the thought of what she could have found, and tried to block that out with reality.

"What're you doing off the ship?" she demanded, voice stern.

The dog was up in an instant, growling at her with its teeth bared.

"Down, girl," Kristof ordered, patting the dog's head. The dog relaxed, though she still cast an untrusting glance Cammie's direction. "She was scared," Kristof explained. "I helped her."

Cammie didn't know what to make of that, so she just turned. "Come on."

"You heard her. Come on, girl," Kristof told the dog, and the two started following her.

"Wait, no." Cammie spun, unable to process that he thought the dog would be coming too. "She's with them. She's one of the enemy."

"No, she's not!" Kristof knelt, wrapping his arm around the dog's neck. "And if she stays, so do I!"

"Everything okay down there?" William called, glancing over the side of the airship with an amused look.

"Looks like we have ourselves a new pet," Cammie said through gritted teeth, then waved Kristof and his new dog forward to join them. "This ought to be a fun one to explain to Royland."

"Thank you thank you thank you," Kristof exclaimed as he and the dog bounded up ahead. There was a small growl as they boarded the ship, but the boy knew how to comfort the dog like Cammie had never seen.

She shook her head at this turn of events and boarded. Near the forward mast, she found the chubby outsider surrounded by her sailors.

"What you want us to do with this guy?" William asked, watching as she stowed the loot. He held a sword to the man's throat.

"He's with us now," she replied, tossing the guy his shirt. It was bloody in places, but it would do. "Name?"

The man looked like he was about to break down crying. "Hines."

"Okay, Hines, whatever the hell kind of name that is." She walked over, took William's sword, and stuck it into the deck. "As long as you play nicely, we won't tear your head off. Got it?"

He looked at her like she was insane, but he nodded.

"Good." She turned back to William and ordered, "Get us airborne. Chubs here's going to tell us where the bad ones are so we can kill them, and where the good ones are so we can schedule some play dates."

Hines closed his eyes and bowed his head, then told them, "I'll do it."

"I know you will," Cammie replied. "I just said so."

"On the condition that you don't kill my family. And...the other families."

"Hines, Hines, Hines." She strode back over to him, lifting his face to look into his eyes. "I'm the good guy here. That means the only people who die are the ones who come after me and mine. Got it?"

He nodded skeptically.

"Well, you will soon enough, if you don't yet." She turned and saw William still standing there, watching in awe, and gave him a look.

"Right, yes." With a wave of his hand he ordered everyone to their positions, and soon they were taking off, following the directions of their newest captive.

Cammie was damn exhausted, so she retreated to the captain's quarters. She knew more trouble was coming, and needed to get some rest.

CHAPTER TWENTY

Toro Inner City

Valerie and Robin spent their evenings watching and observing, occasionally checking in with the others, sometimes staying at the soldier's house. There were two ladies, sisters, actually, they could possibly pass for, though it was a bit of a stretch.

"Notice how she leans slightly to the left," Valerie said, observing the one Robin would impersonate. They stood on the street looking at a menu at the same soup place Valerie had seen that night she had found Robin, while their two potential victims window-shopped across the street.

"A spinal disorder?" Robin asked, sipping her tea, and Valerie gave a slight nod.

They had used their army friend to procure a few generic garments so that they could move about as neither soldier nor slave, though they had to maintain a low profile and keep on the move to avoid anyone asking questions. Toro wasn't exactly a small city, but it was exclusive enough that people would ask questions if they didn't know who you were.

"Val, you sure this'll work?"

"Yes." Valerie smiled, then nodded for them to move so as to seem inconspicuous. They moved forward a bit so that if the ladies noticed them at all it would seem as if they were the ones following.

"I'm sure glad one of us is so positive." Robin adjusted the hem of her dress, a long, beige one. Apparently, women's fashion in Toro had regressed to be quite conservative.

"With the Gathering occurring within the hour, I can't see how any attitude other than positive would help us," Valerie noted. "And in case you forgot—"

"Yes, yes," Robin chuckled, "you're the most amazing thing to walk the Earth."

"I was going to say something about the two of us being unstoppable when we work together, but you're welcome to your opinion."

Robin cast a playful look Valerie's way, then turned to look at the nearly-full moon above. "Tonight... I can't believe it's tonight."

"Come on, let's get in position."

Valerie motioned her to keep up, and together they made their way to the high-end hotel-turned-apartments where the two ladies were staying.

"You don't feel bad about this, do you?" Valerie asked, then moved with vampire speed to shimmy up the side of the hotel and to the window they had figured belonged to the ladies' apartment. She had it open in an instant.

Robin followed, ducking through the open window and landing with a roll. "Me, feel guilty? Not in the slightest. You saw the way these two treated their slaves."

Valerie nodded, moving to check herself in the mirror. She had cleaned up nicely after their travels through the slums and over the last several days had kept up her hygiene. This was a big night, and the last thing she needed was for some soldier to address her in any way, as a slave or soldier, and then recognize her tonight.

"Where do you think these ladies got their dresses, anyway?" Robin asked, pulling them from the closet and laying them out on the bed. They were certainly nice—fancy ball gowns, one dark green and the other lavender—but they had a very old look to them.

"From the dead," Valerie quipped jokingly. Then she cringed, realizing it could in fact be true. But no, more likely they had found old department stores or chests full of clothes or something like that.

"You got issues," Robin stated, sitting on the bed next to the dresses. When she noticed how Valerie was looking at her she cocked her head, leaned back, and bit her lower lip.

Valerie took a step over, hesitant, and then paused at Robin's laugh. "What?"

"Yup, real issues. What were you going to do, make a move on me while we waited for those two? What if they walked in on us?"

"I... Who said I was going to make a move?" Valerie could feel her cheeks flushing. "You looked lonely. I was going to comfort you."

"Uh-huh." Robin lowered one of the shoulders of her beige dress so that the top of her breast was exposed. "How about now? Do I look like I need comforting?"

"Very much so." Valerie laughed. "And you look like a big jerk for teasing me."

Robin stood, came over to Valerie in two long strides, and kissed her passionately. "When this is all over, I promise...no more teasing. Only the real thing."

Valerie gulped, suddenly unable to keep her mind on anything other than Robin's moist lips.

Then her senses kicked in, and she smelled the two ladies' perfume before she heard their voices.

"They're here," she whispered, motioning for Robin to take her place, then moved to the bathroom. They waited, and as soon as the door had closed behind the two sisters and one was starting to comment on wondering who had left the dresses out, the two vampires moved in.

Just like that, it was all over. They didn't kill them, but drained enough blood to leave them woozy and at the edge of consciousness and left them bound in the closet. They would untie them later, or someone would find them. While they were jerks to their slaves, that wasn't quite egregious enough for Valerie to justify killing them.

They quickly changed into their dresses, Valerie doing her best not to look at Robin and tease herself further. However, when she turned to ask if Robin would zip her up, she couldn't help noticing the way Robin was looking at her.

"What?" she asked.

"Just... I've never seen you in a ball gown."

Valerie twirled. "You like?"

"I love it." Robin stepped over and with one hand on her lower back, almost on her ass, she held Valerie in place to zip up the dress. Valerie was about to return the favor when she felt Robin's warm lips on her neck.

"You're just...mean."

Robin pulled back and turned. "My turn."

"Meaning you want me to zip you, or tease you?" Valerie zipped the dress, then stormed off to splash cold water on her face.

"Maybe you'll kill better when you're a little worked up, no?" Robin called from the other room as Valerie quickly applied makeup.

"Maybe we should get out of here before those ladies start kicking the wall and trying to scream," Valerie suggested, walking back out into the main room while drying her hands on a small towel. She almost wanted to keep it—the towel was nicer than any she had seen before—but she tossed it over her shoulder instead.

Robin nodded and then smiled in a way that barely seemed hers at all. She had so much makeup on that Valerie almost thought she was the woman whose identity she was stealing for the night.

The two made their way outside, slowing as they passed the doorman to ensure they were seen.

"You look stunning, Mrs. Tepia, and you too, Mrs. Tepia," the doorman told them, holding the door.

They shared a smile as they exited—if a man who saw them at least twice a day didn't notice anything off about them, they doubted anyone else would. At most, Val figured, he would think they were wearing too much makeup.

Valerie was lucky to have practiced walking in heels many times in her life, but was a bit worried at how Robin kept stumbling.

"You sure you'll be fine?" she asked.

"Shut up and find out where this place is." Robin followed the directions the staff sergeant had given them, and soon they saw others moving toward another hotel that had survived the chaos years.

"Find out who's who, don't draw too much attention to ourselves, and be ready to get out of there and head to the stadium when it's time. We're going to want to be close to the council, if possible, to figure out when and how the coup is happening."

"But it's tonight, yes?"

"That's what we think …"

A man stood at the entryway to the hotel, but just smiled and nodded at them as they entered. Since everyone was in such nice clothes, Valerie's best guess was that everyone here was in the elite class; the rest of society knew the consequences of trying to impersonate one.

They entered to find the ballroom decorated like an old ship, though Valerie thought it more closely resembled an undersea graveyard. Sails hung from the ceiling, and odd bits of flotsam had been used to decorate the walls. Whoever had put this together had spent a lot of time on it, and she was willing to bet it had been the slaves of the town.

In the midst of this parade of people Valerie knew were horrible, at least on whatever level it was that allowed them to operate in a system with slaves, there was one of the most beautiful sights she had seen in quite some time—a band. Back in France there had been music, though not much. She had only seen two live performances ever, and one was on a particularly strange night when the Duke had wanted to celebrate and give his inner circle a treat by playing his clarinet. It was the one time she had felt close to the Duke, the one time she had thought there might be a shred of humanity left in him.

This was different. At the front of the room were several men and women with different stringed instruments, none that she recognized, and they were playing a song with energy, nothing like the melancholy song the Duke had chosen for his so-called celebration.

Several couples had begun to dance, while Valerie and Robin moved to the edge of the room to avoid too much attention.

"We should split up and try to overhear conversations," Valerie whispered. "Figure out who the members of the council are, if they're here."

"I can't see how they wouldn't be," Robin replied. "Something like this? Seems like more of a tribute to them than a mere celebration, if I know anything about how people with power like that work."

Valerie nodded. "Agreed."

"If there's trouble?"

With a glance around the room, Valerie scoffed. "Trouble from these flower petals? I doubt it. But if it comes to it, just get out. We don't want to blow our cover before we've found your parents."

"Agreed."

"And put some of that food in you, please. Honestly, I'm worried."

"I've been kinda saving my appetite for the assholes we're searching for," Robin argued with a playful smile.

"And if you meet them but have no energy?"

Robin rolled her eyes, but nodded.

With that they split paths, Valerie moving to the side with the band, Robin heading the other way toward the tables with plates of food laid out. From here Valerie could smell the almond-crusted fish, though she didn't know fish well enough to know what kind, and platters of roast vegetables. As her eyes roamed the crowd she wondered what feasts would have been like in the old days when these lands were said to have had vastly differing seasons and vegetation. Back when cows inhabited the fields in great numbers and factories supposedly pumped out chickens and even experimented with new ways to create meat.

Of course, none of that might have been real, for all she knew.

A man walked among the throng, and as he passed the men and women would slightly inch away or turn to nod. When he stopped to engage a couple in conversation, Valerie couldn't help but notice the way they mostly averted their gaze and waited for his lead.

She took a few steps closer, pretending to admire the string of shells lining a glass sculpture, and used her enhanced hearing to listen in.

"It's all very glamorous," the woman declared.

"But you're really here for the after-party, aren't you?" the important man asked. "The Games will be like nothing we've ever had here, like only those in ancient times would even begin to know the greatness of." The couple waited a moment, and then the important man chuckled. "It's okay, ask away."

"Is it...true?" the man asked.

"About the vampires, we mean," the woman added, her voice subdued to the point that Valerie almost couldn't hear her.

"You'll have to be surprised like everyone else," the important man told them with a wink that Valerie caught out of the corner of her eye.

He excused himself and walked on. Valerie was considering following him when she heard a laugh. Robin's laugh. She turned, looking for the woman, and spotted her on the dance floor, a man turning her. It was almost humorous, knowing how much work was going into making it look natural, but at the same time it was disturbing. She was supposed to listen in, not become the center of attention. Other people were looking, too. Several gave cautious glances, and there were murmurs of interest and confusion.

"Madam Luroy will have a fit over this," a woman whispered to her partner.

"What is he thinking?" another asked.

Clearly this wasn't a smart move for various reasons. When she turned to get closer and hear what was happening, she found an older woman in a flowing red dress standing there with her hands folded before her. She wore a smile, but the aura coming from her was pure fire.

"First you, now your sister?" the woman spat.

"Excuse me?"

The woman didn't look at her, which was probably good considering she apparently knew the two women Valerie and Robin were impersonating.

"You two keep this up, you might find yourself wearing different clothes in the future." She made a clicking noise in the back of her throat, and then turned to meander off to some other part of the party.

Valerie had to get in there and see what was so important, so when she saw a man glance her way she allowed a hint of a smile.

He approached and held his hand out. "May I have this dance?"

"Here I was thinking you'd never ask," she replied, holding out her hand for him to take her to the dance floor.

This was certainly not in her comfort zone but she did well enough, able to make up for awkward movements with vampire balance and grace. He twirled her and she allowed him to lead for a moment, then subtly drew them closer to Robin.

"I've seen you around," the man stated. "It's a shame we haven't had a chance to talk before."

Valerie smiled, pretending to look shy while in reality focusing her hearing on Robin and her dance partner.

"Those days are long gone," Robin's partner was saying. "It's a time for a rebirth, an age of Toro's majesty."

"You sound positively in love with this city," Robin replied in a soothing voice.

"Hell, who could help but be?" He spun her and Valerie lost a moment of the conversation as her partner blabbed on about himself, something about how the council had marked him for great things, and then she saw that older lady glaring at Robin again, this time accompanied by two very important men.

Valerie maneuvered toward Robin, causing her dance partner to bump into someone in the process. While he was apologizing and the others were distracted, she hissed, "What're you doing?"

Robin quickly replied, "He seemed to know me, insisted we dance."

"You're causing trouble." Valerie nodded over to the older woman, but by then the others had recovered from the little incident and began dancing again.

Only something was off—a scent that Valerie knew.

As she let the man spin her, she homed in on it—one of the two men the older lady was talking to was definitely a Forsaken. His nose twitched, and she saw his eyes widen and then dart over the dance floor.

She finished her spin and then politely excused herself before his eyes could land on her, though she was pretty sure he'd spotted Robin when he froze, eyes narrowed. Valerie threaded through the crowd, eyes still on him, and noted which door he left through when he turned and took off.

With a wave to Robin and then a finger that said she'd be back in one minute, Valerie headed toward the door. Running in this dress and the shoes was a pain, but she was soon through the doors and darting down the hall—except he wasn't there.

She checked a couple of the side doors and even paused to sniff to catch his scent, but he had vanished. The vampire had clearly been talking with members of the council, at least two, she guessed, which meant she now had a good idea who was in on the coup.

But the vampire was free, and knew about Robin for sure. He might have sensed Valerie as well and not shown it.

At least she knew who to keep an eye on.

This time when she returned to the ball she stayed back, watching the older lady and the man she had seen with the Forsaken. Without a doubt, those two were up to something as they moved about the room talking with other key individuals. They were either conspiring, she thought, or doing their best to assure the others that they weren't.

This continued for some time until finally Robin excused herself and nodded to a back door almost imperceptibly; just enough for Valerie to notice. Valerie went there first, to be followed a few minutes later by Robin.

"I hope that was worth it," Valerie hissed when they were alone in a back hallway. "Did you learn anything?"

Robin nodded. "I learned people here have issues, for one. The guy tried to get me to go with him. Said we didn't have long before they would call us all to the Games, but that we could make it work."

"Slimeball." Valerie cocked her head. "He wasn't bad-looking though, was he?"

"Shut up." Robin added, "I'm not going to stroke your ego or insecurity or whatever that just was."

Valerie chuckled. "Okay, fine. So we know the Games will be soon."

"And that was a bit ago, so probably not long now."

"Did you see the Forsaken?" Valerie asked.

Robin's eyes went wide. "I…is that what it was? My sense of smell isn't nearly as good as yours."

"He got away, though."

"And what would you have done if you had caught him?"

Valerie shrugged. "Questioned him, I guess? Maybe beat him to a pulp."

"And alerted the others that something was up before it was time."

"Damn." Valerie rubbed her forehead, realizing it was a good thing that she hadn't caught up with him. "Well, point is, there's a lady in there who has it in for us. I think she has some connection to the man you were dancing with, and I think the other versions of us have some history there that pisses her off. Also, she's connected with the Forsaken."

"So she means to overthrow some other council member," Robin speculated. "We need to keep our eyes on her during the Games, whatever the hell they are."

"Agreed."

They returned to the room, staying out of sight this time while being careful to move about and, just when someone looked like they might come over or say something, disappear. The older lady kept mingling, while the man she had been with kept to himself. He was a large man with thinning hair, and was wearing an olive suit.

"How many Forsaken do you think they have?" Robin asked.

"Could just be the one, but I'm guessing they've struck some deal, this lady and the Forsaken, so there're probably more."

Robin stared into the distance, lost in her thoughts. "It just… seems odd that so many of those bastards have survived this long."

"Not really. Don't forget that there're a lot of Nosferatu, or so they say. If that's true, it indicates to me that one or two strong Forsaken set out to breed new vampires. The failed attempts led to Nosferatu, and the successful ones meant more Forsaken to rely on in the struggle against good."

Not much happened for a time, and soon Valerie found herself wishing they really *were* at a dance like this, without fake identities or the risk of all that was going on around them. Dances like this didn't come around too often, and she would have loved to have taken advantage of it.

"If we ever go back to New York," Valerie asked, "What do you say to starting an annual ball?"

Robin looked at her uneasily.

"I said *if*." Valerie wanted to reach out and take her hand, but knew how that would look here. "I mean, there's a possibility, maybe."

"Is there?" Robin glanced at her, eyes full of doubt. "Let's assume we find my parents and they want to go there. What are the chances you could ever settle down? I mean, didn't you say you faked your own death in New York?"

Valerie swallowed, only now remembering that little fact.

"It's not like you could be out and about after that, or maybe you could explain it away, I don't know…but what about the rest of the world?"

"You mean, with everything going on in the world, people out there committing evil, others in need of a Justice Enforcer, could I just…go into retirement?"

"Well, could you?"

Dammit, thinking about the answer to that question hurt Valerie's brain, but it hurt her heart even more. As much as the answer was clear, she had somewhere deep down hoped that a normal life might someday be possible for her. Now that Robin had voiced it, though, there was no doubt in Valerie's mind that she wouldn't be able to rest until the world was at peace.

And there was still the idea that she could go into space and be part of the bigger battle to keep Earth safe. If the threats from out there had occupied the Queen Bitch all this time, there was certainly a big enough threat to make Valerie useful out there as well.

With a sorrow-filled glance at Robin, she shook her head.

"That's what I thought." Robin smiled, but there was no doubt it was forced. "I knew it would be like that, or at least I'd started to realize it. It's why I haven't let you get too close. Why we haven't, well…"

"I get it." Valerie wasn't sure if she wanted to shred this whole ball or run away in tears. The feeling of unease in her gut met the pain in her chest, but both were pushed aside by the part of her brain that had known this was coming.

It wasn't like they would stop being close or that this mission was over yet by any means, but she was pretty sure that she and Robin had just broken up, if they had ever really been together.

Part of her said it was okay and that it wasn't so much a breakup as a realization that her true love, the only love that could stick with her in the long run, was her love of humanity. To fight for what was right. To stand for justice and ensure evil met its demise.

She was searching for something to say to let Robin know that it was all fine and dandy when a bell sounded, causing her to notice that the band had stopped.

"Let the Games commence!" a man shouted, stepping in front of the band and motioning toward the doors.

"Time to see what this is all about." Robin gave her a fleeting smile before heading for the doors, and Valerie followed a second later.

CHAPTER TWENTY-ONE

Toro Inner City

It was a strange sight, Robin thought. All these men and women in their fancy dresses piling into the stadium that, on all other sides, up and down, were filled with people in all manner of dress from the brown slave clothes to everyday shirts and jeans to some that looked as though they had come from the slums, though Valerie insisted that wasn't likely.

They were ushered in with the rest of the elite, and they found seating in the old section of the stadium that was crumbling at the top. At one edge part of the old white roof still clung desperately to the walls, but looked as if it could give at any minute.

First chance they got, the two slipped away. Valerie had whispered what seemed obvious, once they thought about it—there would be a fight. They had heard enough rumors to know it, and that just made sense when there were public games of any sort in this world.

They darted around the crowds, making sure to find a hallway at the bottom not occupied other than by two soldiers.

"Gentlemen, which way to the bathrooms?" Valerie asked, looking stunning in her gown.

The guy just grunted and pointed, but before he could turn away or bother to check her out, she had moved and taken out him and the other soldier. Valerie motioned to Robin.

"Hurry, if we're going to potentially crash these games, we should be prepared." Valerie checked around the corner and dragged the two men to the wall and out of view, then quickly removed their clothes and body armor and handed it to Robin.

As she took it, Robin noticed the other guy didn't have body armor, just shoulder protectors.

"You take it," she said, trying to push the body armor back.

Valerie scoffed. "Shut up and put it on. We both know I don't need it."

"Who says I do?" Robin asked.

"Me. Probably your parents, if you were to ask them."

Robin hesitated, pursed her lips in thought, and then tossed off her gown and began to dress like the soldier.

Valerie did the same, though when it came to putting on his camouflage top, it was obviously too big. She tossed it aside and stood there in the army pants, a tank top, and the shoulder guards.

Robin laughed. "Sorry, but you look kind of ridiculous. Who would honestly wear that into battle?"

With a shrug, Valerie flipped her hair back. "I'm thinking of starting a new fashion trend."

"I'm sure the guys will like it, with your breasts practically popping out of that tank top. Just…put something over it."

"And look like a kid in her grandpa's clothes?" Valerie scoffed. "I'd rather go for sexy. More distracting that way."

"Whatever you say." Robin shook her head. "So what now? We fit in with the soldiers around the stands, pretend we're on duty."

"Precisely. It's not like we care about getting caught."

"Sounds peachy," Robin replied, and then motioned to Valerie to lead the way.

They worked their way up the stairs and found an area separate from where the elites had been seated, but close enough in case they had a reason to leap back up there quickly.

"I'd hate to be under that," Robin stated, then lowered her eyes to see that the entire area below the partial roof was filled with slaves. "Fuck me."

"Your parents might not be there," Valerie noted, seemingly reading her mind.

Robin nodded absently, straining her vampire eyes to see if she could find them among the crowd. While she could make out faces fairly well, there were too many of them, some blocked.

She didn't give up even when the announcer walked out onto the field.

"Ladies and gentlemen," the announcer shouted into a microphone that actually worked, to Robin's surprise. His voice echoed through the stadium. "Today we bring you back to days of old. We're not talking just pre-collapse, we're talking the dawn of civilization as those people knew it. Today you'll be treated to a gladiatorial display unlike anything anyone has ever seen. Because today we give you...*vampires!*"

The crowd erupted in a mixture of confusion and disbelief.

Robin turned from the crowd of slaves to Valerie, whose eyes were wide. The elite above them were cheering; all but the older woman from the ball, who sat with a smug smile on her scrunched-up little face.

Robin leaned into Valerie. "What's this vampires business, do you think?"

"Since I doubt they're on to us..." Valerie pointed with a groan. "Yes, right there. See for yourself."

Robin followed her finger and felt her mouth going dry. These people not only knew about vampires—or Nosferatu, to be more precise—they were going to pit them against each other for entertainment?

No wonder the local Forsaken were eager to take part in a coup. These were their creations, their minions, in a sense. How could the leaders of Toro have accomplished this?

"They're in on it," Valerie murmured, voice hushed.

"What?"

"The Forsaken. There's something here we're not seeing. This wouldn't happen without the Forsaken being part of it."

Robin leaned forward in her chair, realizing that Valerie was right. Why would the Forsaken allow their Nosferatu to fight each other for entertainment?

As she watched the announcer open another door into the arena, she understood that she had been wrong. It wasn't about them fighting each other.

The rumors she had heard came flashing back—that this was about removing the older slaves from the population. It hadn't seemed possible, or maybe it had seemed too cruel, so she had dismissed it. But there they were—a group of slaves being herded onto the field below, opposite the Nosferatu.

"And now," the announcer was saying, gesturing as someone pulled a rope to remove the cloth cover from a table of weapons, "in Round One, we will demonstrate what happens when untrained humans go up against these creatures of the night."

The slaves, still bound by chains, were pointed toward the weapons. Some ran for them, others stared around in confusion, and one started beseeching the crowd.

Robin started to stand, but Valerie put a hand on her leg.

"Do you see your parents?" Valerie asked.

Again Robin strained her eyes, but shook her head. Nothing. She did, however, notice Martha and Rand in the crowd to their right among the normal people, and was pleased to see several others they had rescued from Slaver's Peak.

She nodded to Valerie. "We've got backup."

Valerie glanced over. "Good. And our friend?"

Robin shot a quick glance at the older woman; she wasn't there. "Gone."

"Which means something's going to happen to the others here, I'd imagine."

"My parents are likely somewhere in the crowd. Either way, if we don't act now those men and women down there will die."

"You're prepared to blow our cover to ensure that doesn't happen?"

Robin considered and then simply said, "Yes."

"Who am I to stick to plans when people's lives are on the line?"

With a leap, Valerie was out of the seats and then running down the aisle stairs. Robin didn't waste any time and was soon following her. Gasps and shouts of confusion sounded as they ran past.

The announcer had just shouted, *"LET THE GAMES COMMENCE"* and darted from the field when Robin and Valerie reached the ledge that separated the stadium from the seats. The Nosferatu had been released and the chains of the slaves had dropped, but people were starting to notice Valerie and Robin.

"You two, back up!" the announcer yelled and someone else was on the microphone screaming at them, but they weren't listening because the Nosferatu were already moving.

One of the slaves had charged forward and the crowd screamed as the Nosferatu swept over him, devouring him, blood spraying. More moved to the other slaves, but Valerie and Robin were darting forward, putting everything into it, and Valerie was shouting for the slaves to stay back.

Robin glanced at Martha and the others and held up a hand to tell them not to move yet. She could take care of this with Valerie.

"Mind if I borrow that?" she shouted as she darted past one of the slaves, snatching the machete from his hand.

The Nosferatu were almost upon them. Two steps later,

Robin connected. She leaped into the air and brought down the blade to hack through the creature's neck, sending its head flying.

Screams came from the crowd, some already trying to run away, but men with guns appeared, ordering them to stay seated.

Valerie tore through the enemy like they were paper dolls, slamming them with her shoulder guards and ripping them to shreds with her long claws. A couple managed to throw attacks her way, resulting in tears to the tank top, but nothing more. It was quite the sight—all that beauty turned into a ball of rage and destruction.

Robin spun for her next attack, then her next, and soon this group of Nosferatu was finished.

Valerie and Robin stood there, chests heaving, covered in blood. The slaves backed away, but the announcer leaped up onto a stage. He wore a white suit and had on a black cowboy hat, and a bracelet or fancy watch shimmered in the moonlight as he pointed at them.

"It seems we have some new contenders for you all tonight," his voice boomed from the sound system. "That being the case, we thought we'd switch to the main event."

Robin didn't like the sound of that but she simply turned, looking for any sign of her parents.

A gate toward the back of the stadium moved down with a screeching, followed by a large group of slaves running in while shots were fired behind them.

And there they were—first her mom, eyes wide with fright, looking much older than Robin remembered her. Next her dad appeared, wrapping an arm around her mom and whispering something while holding a hand out as if to push the others away.

Their eyes met Robin's with a mixture of confusion, relief, and terror.

She darted forward, hugging them, and the announcer hooted. "Look at that, ladies and gentlemen, our new contenders seem to have a soft spot for slaves. That's going to make this next part very tough, then."

"Stay close!" Robin shouted, grasping her parents by the shoulders, barely able to believe they were here with her after all this time. "Whatever happens, I'll keep you safe."

"That's what a father should be saying to his daughter," her dad replied. "I just…how? Where have you been?"

"Looking for you, Dad." She kissed them each on the cheek, and then the shots started.

"We love you, dear," her mom told her between screams as they ran. "Whatever happens next, never forget that."

"Nothing's going to happen to you two!" Robin called, getting between them and the shots, head swiveling back and forth to search for the shooters.

Slaves dropped dead at the periphery, then others started running and screaming away from the gates.

Robin and her parents were moving too—if for no other reason than to avoid being trampled—and then she saw where the shots were coming from.

Those machines she had seen the soldiers putting together, if you could call them that. It looked like metal walls coming at them with several gun ports and even holes for blades and spears. They were barely held off the ground by the antigrav technology, and it looked like a couple people ran alongside them, the antigrav letting them push them with ease, while others had seated shooting positions on the machines themselves.

"Fucking turtles!" her dad shouted.

"Turtles? Oh, like you taught me, back in Ancient Rome."

"It's what they had us working on. We were underground, but—"

More shots interrupted him and they dove to the ground.

"Tell me more…afterwards." She turned to look for Valerie. "Val!"

Valerie was there in an instant. "You take the one on the right."

Robin looked between her and her parents, shaking her head. "I have to protect them."

"How many others will die if you don't do something?"

Robin looked at her mom and dad, and knew it was true. "Stay down."

She jumped up, prepared herself, and then ran for the turtle on the right. The rifles started firing, but instead of leaping out of the way to avoid getting hit she took the shots. No way was she going to let those bullets pass her and risk them hitting her parents. But that made her think and, as she saw Valerie leap over the one on the left, she made an arc around hers so that its back was exposed as it turned to follow her.

They shot more, and when she got close, jabbed with their spears and swords through slits in the metal.

Had they been fighting against Forsaken or Nosferatu the turtle might have proven to be a problem, but as it was, Valerie was too damn good for them.

Robin felt the *push* of fear as Valerie let loose. Even though she had grown used to it to a degree and learned to mostly block its affects, she took a step back and cringed. The others felt it worse, and even the audience fell into a hush.

One of the slaves maneuvering the turtle closest to Robin took off running and then the other one fell as Valerie darted around the machine and dove in, plucking its operators away and flinging them onto the field.

All but the soldier operating the main gun, the one who tried to turn and stab her. Blood splattered the ground and Robin lost sight of them as the audience let out a gasp.

"She's one of them!" someone shouted even as Robin moved in take down the second turtle.

"Both of them!" another confirmed. "They're vampires!"

As if on cue, more gates opened and a new group of

Nosferatu came charging in. Not just onto the field, though; the section where the elite sat was suddenly swarming with Nosferatu, who sank their teeth into those well-dressed pompous asses.

Robin finished off a soldier as she turned, debating her next move. The elite were in trouble, but the slaves, including her parents, were squaring off with the Nosferatu down here.

She knew her place. It was with her family.

With a war cry, she charged the Nosferatu. Out of the corner of her eye, she saw Valerie waving for Martha and the others to join in and shouted, "Save as many as you can," though Robin doubted whether they could hear her.

There wasn't time to worry about the elite, though. None of that other stuff mattered when she saw her dad backing up, pushing her mom behind him as he held up a metal bar he must've found among the weapons.

One of the Nosferatu was almost upon him, but Robin leaped forward and tackled it mid-jump. They landed in a roll, during which she dropped the machete. Robin recovered, tore off one of her heels, and jammed it into the beast's eye socket. She slammed it deeper with the heel of her hand, and the Nosferatu stopped moving.

She stood, kicking off the other shoe so that it whapped the next Nosferatu in the head, pulling its attention from the crowd of slaves.

With a quick roll to grab the machete, she came up swiftly hacking at the Nosferatu's midsection, spilling its guts, then jammed the blade deep into its skull. When she tried to pull the blade free it snapped in half, but she punted and sunk the half-blade deep into the mouth of the next one.

She turned to see that Valerie had taken out more than her fair share, and a couple of the Nosferatu had turned and fled. Martha and her pirates were holding off the Nosferatu in the stands, though many of the elite had already fallen.

That's when she noticed the men and women in the top row,

six in all, struggling to hold their own. Two Forsaken emerged from the walkway behind them, eyes glowing red, and made their move, sinking their teeth into the members of the council.

Screams filled the arena as those who hadn't yet figured out what was happening did so, and now everyone was in a panic. Some ran while soldiers turned their guns on them, and others tried to make it to the arena floor.

The council was evil as far as Robin knew, but so was anyone who could betray them and give their lives to vampires.

As far as she was concerned, that battle wasn't hers. She was here for her parents, nothing more.

Backing up to them, her father kissed the side of her head.

"What'd they do to you?" he asked. "Are you like...a super-soldier?"

"A mutant?" her mom asked.

"A bit of both, in a way," Robin replied, hugging them while looking for the best exit. "I'm one of them. I'm a vampire. Only difference is, I have another vampire friend who's stronger than all of them."

They looked at her with confusion, but she motioned to Valerie just as she took over one of the turtles, maneuvering it all by herself. With the antigrav and her vampire strength the turtle moved through the air like a glider, landing on the stands just next to the two vampires. She put a couple bullets in each of them, then stepped back and used it like a massive baseball bat. She connected with the first one and sent him flying, then leaped forward to destroy the second with her bare hands.

The armed slaves converged on the vampire who had fallen among them, and it was soon over for him.

"Enough!" a woman's voice shouted, and they all turned to see the older council woman at the microphone.

"Lady Regent." Robin's father instinctively bowed his head, though he stopped when he noticed his daughter giving him a confused glance.

With a wave of her hand, Lady Regent had all of the soldiers aiming their guns into the arena, ready to take down all of the slaves along with Robin. Some in the stands were aiming at Valerie, which would have made Robin want to laugh if she weren't so worried for her parents.

"These vampires have come here to destroy our city!" Lady Regent shouted into the microphone. "They have killed the other council members, and if they aren't stopped, they'll devour us all!"

Shouts of panic continued, but some had turned at this, erupting with rage. Apparently this woman had some sway over these people.

"*Wrong!*" Valerie shouted from the stands, voice carrying with almost as much power as if she were using the microphone. "We've uncovered a plot by this woman to overthrow your council with the help of evil vampires, the ones we call Forsaken. But we would have overthrown the council regardless, so..." She turned to the lady. "I have to thank you, and now kindly ask you to step down."

Lady Regent laughed, motioning at all the soldiers with guns, at all the people in the stands. "These are my people. They will follow me into death."

"Is that so?" Valerie took a few steps down the stands as she spoke. "Are the slaves your people too? How about those you have tossed into the slums?" Valerie raised her hands, and the people hushed. "There is no room for elite and slaves in this new world. Your time has come. The people of Toro...no, *Toronto*, have a choice to make." She turned to address the crowd, slaves and others alike. "Do you choose to live under her whip, or stand in a world where justice is paramount, where there are no slaves, no men or women like her telling you that you are lesser humans? *You* make the choice!"

A long silence followed, during which Robin imagined

everyone was deciding where they belonged, which side they would take.

"Who is she?" Robin's mom asked, almost in a whisper.

"My dear friend," Robin replied, feeling a chill of excitement run through her arms. "

"Then we're with her." Her dad stepped forward, metal bar raised, as he shouted, "We won't live in your chains any longer!"

Others cheered and charged even as shots were fired into the crowd of slaves. But soon the direction of the shooting had changed as some soldiers fired on the others. Robin spotted Brody leading the counterattack and then saw Martha again, tackling a soldier and pulling his gun free. She tossed him from the stands.

Lady Regent glared and took a step back from the stage, signaling. A line of those metal turtles formed before her, and then she was running.

Valerie was gone in a flash, followed by a spray of blood. The turtles drifted aside, since the soldiers operating them were dead. Slaves ran forward to take them over and turned on any soldiers who tried to make a move, while Valerie ran after Lady Regent.

A moment later, a loud *oomph* sounded, followed by a shape flying through the air and landing with a thud and a small bounce not far from Robin.

Valerie was there a moment later, and when everyone saw that it was Lady Regent who had been thrown and now lay on the ground struggling to pick herself up, the other fighting came to a halt.

"This is the leader who betrayed you," Valerie informed them, standing beside Robin. "Your other leaders are dead or dying; she saw to that. But now you can all lead together. We're not here to tell you how to run this place. We tell you only that you will not take slaves, and you will try to live to the best of your ability in ways that help rather than hurt those around you." She turned to Robin. "This woman, my friend, was taken by vampires against her will, and made into one. That does not make her evil. Her parents were also taken and sold into slavery, and now they are together again."

A cheer rose from the slaves, with some cheering scattered throughout other parts of the crowd as well.

Valerie nodded, then added, "I would ask your permission to let her determine this woman's fate."

Robin's heart skipped a beat. She looked at Valerie in confusion, but only got a smile of confidence in return.

When silence followed, Valerie turned to Robin and held out a hand. "What'll it be?"

Robin looked at her mom and dad, then at the woman on the ground. Lady Regent glared back with gritted teeth, blood starting to seep out of her arm where the fall had broken a bone.

This woman was broken, the city no longer hers.

As much as Robin wanted revenge, that wasn't her way. She stepped forward, projecting her voice as Valerie had done. "You will be imprisoned. Your days manipulating others are done, and any here who attempt to follow your path will join you. We will launch an investigation to find those who would attempt to break you free, and they will join you as well. Does this work for everyone?"

Shouts of agreement rose, and Robin turned back to her parents, relieved that was over.

Her mom smiled and held out her arms, then froze. The smile turned to a shout of *"No!"*

As Robin spun, she heard the click of the pistol and saw the explosion as the bullet left the chamber, and then Valerie was there, swatting the bullet aside with the back of her hand.

In an instant she was on Lady Regent, teeth bared at her neck, eyes glowing red.

"Are you still certain?" Valerie asked. "Because if you've changed your mind…"

Robin considered it and then stepped forward, picking up the gun from the ground and checking to see that there was a round in the chamber.

"To ensure this doesn't happen again…" She lowered the pistol and fired, putting two holes in Lady Regent's left hand and then two in her right, firing so fast the woman didn't have time to react before it was over.

As Lady Regent screamed, Robin nodded to a couple of the now-freed slaves. "You know what? Fuck it. That's my preference, but you all do whatever the hell you want with her."

The slaves smiled at that, and dragged her out of there.

"Way to be a leader." Valerie smirked.

"Hey, I never claimed to be a leader or a person who makes decisions like that," Robin said. "In fact—hell, no! I refuse. All I ever wanted was my family back."

Valerie nodded. "Fair enough." She turned to the audience and shouted, "People of Toronto, this city is yours once again!"

As the celebration commenced, Valerie and Robin walked out of there with Robin's parents. Valerie waved for Martha and the others to meet them outside, while Robin just wrapped her arms around her parents, never wanting to let go.

Leaving the town of Toronto behind was both a relief and a tough call for Valerie. On the one hand, she wanted to stay here and see that it was set right, but she knew that her long-term mission to dole out justice and ensure the world wasn't ruled by tyrants meant she couldn't stay in every city she liberated. Would evil rise again? It was possible, but she was hopeful that putting the right people in the right positions would alleviate that concern.

That was why, when Robin's parents had volunteered to stay and help set Toronto right, it had made so much sense to her.

But when Robin turned, eyes on the ground, and told her,

"I'm staying too," it had felt like a silver dagger plunging into Valerie's chest.

"I don't... I don't understand," Valerie replied, standing at the outskirts of the city and looking back at the dome and the spear-looking building. She wondered how Robin could possibly want to make this place home. "What about justice? Making the world a safer place and all that?"

Robin shook her head, taking Valerie by the hand and walking away from the others a few paces. "Dear, that was always you. Did I want to help? Yes. But right now I just want to be with my family, and maybe make a difference here. I can make sure that there're no other groups of Nosferatu around, establish a foundation here. Who knows? Maybe someday we'll be ready to move south, join New York or something."

"But... New York isn't my home."

Robin nodded, then dropped Valerie's hand as she folded her own in front of her. "I know, Val. Right now, this is what's best. I told you that, basically. We discussed it, and you knew it was coming."

"I know, but that doesn't mean it hurts any less." She turned, looking at the ships waiting for them; the people who would sail with her to fight for those in need. She could stay here too. But that wasn't who she was, and part of her had to admit that this whole relationship had felt like a bit of a dream anyway. She had left France a vampire who had lived a long life relative to humans, but had no relationships. Now she could say she had two, and better understood who she was. She understood her need to focus, to stand for justice and not be distracted by matters of the heart. As much as that sucked, she glanced at Robin and reminded herself how such thoughts could cause her to wander from the path. How many people would suffer if she let such feelings dissuade her from her calling?

Maybe there'd be room for all that relationship stuff in her future, but not now.

"I'll be fine," Valerie told her, smiling again. "And so will you and your parents. I believe in you."

"Thank you, Val. For everything."

Valerie was about to leave when Robin threw her arms around her. They held each other, Valerie breathing in the sweet honey scent of Robin—possibly for the last time. It was different, as if changing with Robin's moods? Maybe it was because she was closer to her parents now, and hopeful. Or maybe she had simply bathed.

"Send word to Cleveland, Chicago and the others," Valerie asked. "Let them know Toro has fallen and Toronto is back in play."

"I will."

Valerie held her a moment longer, then sighed and muttered, "Fuck, I'll miss you."

Robin smiled and rolled her eyes. "You'll be too busy kicking ass to give a damn."

With a laugh, Valerie nodded, then turned and walked off to join her crew. With a final thought, she paused and looked back.

"I don't know when, but if I go to space, and if you're around then, I could use someone with your skills at my side."

"I'll keep that in mind," Robin replied.

Finally, Valerie left and didn't look back. When she reached the ships, she found a surprise waiting for her.

"We thought you might like that," one of the women announced, beaming.

"Hell yes, I do," Valerie replied, stepping up to the side of her airship, tracing the large design they had carved into the hull. It was a vampire skull over crossbones, bat wings on each side. While she didn't have bat wings—another part of some old legends about vampires—it was perfect.

Rand stepped forward. "What'll it be?"

"Let's sail!" she called, and her followers shouted a cheer before moving in to prepare the airships for takeoff.

CHAPTER TWENTY-TWO

Old Canada

The fighting itself wasn't the fun part for Cammie. It was the thrill just before the fight when all the adrenalin was running through her. Killing for the sake of killing was barbaric. Proving herself against someone trying to take her life, however, made simple sense.

From where she stood, she felt there had been enough proving herself for three lifetimes.

Over the last week they had made a large dent in the locals' claim to a land where anything goes. That wasn't going to be the way of it; they needed the rule of law, and they needed people to be accountable for their actions. It was the only way the land could rebuild in a civilized fashion.

But this group standing before her seemed to be the worst. All the pirates who had vanished from Prince Edward Island and not gone with the Prince were here, along with a hodgepodge of others. They had apparently heard she was coming, because they had thrown together a wall of old cars, metal spikes, concertina wire, and anything else they could get their hands on.

If there was one thing she was sure of, it was that they would all die if they continued down this path.

With a sigh, she realized that she didn't want them to die.

"You have your history, your past," she shouted, stepping forward, hands out to show she meant no harm. "That does *not* have to define who you will be in the future."

Several heads stuck up from behind the wall under a sign that read "Welcome to." It had the bottom half blacked out, replaced with spray paint so that it said, "*HELL!*"

"You're the one, right?" a woman shouted. "The one they're calling the devil?"

"If I were, would this be my home? Would you be my welcome committee?"

The woman stared at her in confusion, clearly having forgotten the sign was there.

Cammie shook her head. "No, I'm no devil. Are they calling me that now? Not long ago that was a title some gave my good friend Valerie. If it has been transferred to me, I'd say it's an honor. But do I condone evil? Far from it."

"Is she or isn't she?" a man next to the woman asked.

"Hell if I know, she's going on about some bullshit," the woman answered.

Cammie wanted to facepalm but instead shouted, "You can't stick to the old ways anymore. It's time you joined civilization."

"We choose freedom."

Cammie glanced back at the people aboard the airship. William was there, ready with his rifle, the others nearby with other weapons. No, it wasn't time for that.

"Listen to me very carefully." Cammie took another step closer to the compound. "Men and women have fought for generations using the word freedom as their excuse. Fuck that. *I fight for freedom*. Freedom for children to grow up without the threat of violence or death by some asshole, or worse. Freedom from dickheads who would like to take what's mine without permission, and freedom to relax in peace with the person I love, knowing that we won't have to shed blood ever again. You want freedom? If your freedom stands in opposition to mine, if you want freedom to rape and pillage, to practice cannibalism and do whatever the hell you want...then fuck you. If that's you, you're going to die today. The rest of you need to join me on my airship or find some other way of getting to Prince Edward Island, where we're building a society of the free. *My* kind of free."

There was a long pause, and then the woman disappeared. Cammie heard shouting from two more voices, a man and a woman arguing that they couldn't go out there, that someone by the name of Big D would slaughter them all, and then there was a gunshot, followed by another.

Cammie shifted uneasily, then readied herself as a metal grating sound came from the side of the improvised wall, followed by a door opening. The woman from above stepped out, followed by a dozen men and women and four children.

They approached her cautiously, stopping a few paces away.

There was a smoking pistol in the woman's hand.

"I take it there were two of you who didn't like the idea of coming out here?" Cammie asked.

"Don't none of us like it," the woman answered. "We don't know if we can trust you, but you speak language that sure sounds like the truth, so we made a choice. You turn out to be some serial-killer son-of-a-bitch or worse, I swear I'll gut you myself. We've got kids here, kids I mean to see to adulthood."

A broad-shouldered man stepped up behind the woman, hand on a blade in his belt. "We're not so proud that we can't see reason."

"Good," Cammie replied, and then froze at the sound of shouting from inside the compound. "And that would be?"

"Big D," the woman responded. "He has another fifty or so fighters in there, men mostly, who won't be coming so easily."

"Truth be told," the man added, "we heard more about you

than your dark side, and were ready to come over if you assured us the good rumors were true. You mostly did."

Cammie nodded, focusing on the compound in case anyone started firing. "Get the children to the ship and tell my fighters to get their asses ready."

"Don't need to tell us twice." The woman motioned for one of the younger men to go. He started off with the kids, but the others stayed.

"Go on then," Cammie commanded. "What're you waiting for?"

The woman turned and lifted the back of her shirt to show fresh blood in streaks. "Devil lady, I know you're going to teach Big D a lesson in humility, hopefully introduce him to Lady Death herself, but I'll be damned if I ain't going to get mine. That boy needs a whupping, and I mean to help give that to him."

Cammie smiled. "Shit, I'm liking you already. What's your name?"

"Bertha," the woman said with a smile that revealed three gold teeth. *"Fucking Bertha* if you're pissed at me, Fucking Bertha if you play your cards right."

A laugh escaped Cammie's mouth and she nodded. Yup, this woman would fit in just fine.

"What've we got?" William asked, running up to join them. The other fighters were right behind him.

"Some jackhole who calls himself Big D," Cammie replied.

William scoffed. "Wow, sounds like a fun guy to kill."

"Likely."

Bertha glanced at the ship, then at the wall, and Cammie guessed what she was thinking.

"He prepared for a land attack, but not one from the air, am I right?" Cammie folded her arms across her chest, smiling when Bertha nodded. "Oooh, this is going to be that much more fun."

They went back to the airship and heard cheers from the compound as the remaining fighters must have assumed Cammie and the others were in retreat. That made it even more fun when Cammie had William take them up and start sailing for the fortress.

"Get her out of range," she commanded. "And ready the ropes."

"If we're out of range the ropes won't be long enough," he shouted from the control room.

"A wolf can land from quite a distance," she replied. "When the shooting stops, you lower the ship. Oh, and get the kids into the secure hold."

The shooting started moments later, but the extra plating on the airship that had made their travel slower proved its worth. Shot after shot pinged off the ship, not doing a bit of damage.

Whatever she had been before back in the days of the Golden City and as a Hunter, that was an old her that was gone, and she felt it. This new her had a purity flowing through her blood, a connection with Valerie, maybe even with Bethany Anne and the greats of old. She wasn't here by anyone else's command, but for the higher power of honor and justice. She was here to protect the weak and punish evil.

Fuck, it felt good.

Now she understood why Valerie always seemed so secure in herself, so at peace with who she was. She had a purpose, and that purpose was clear.

"Remember, when the shots stop hitting the ship, that means go!" she shouted as she ran, leaping over the side of the ship and grabbing a rope.

Yeah, it hurt like hell as she slid down, the rope burning the palms of her hands. But it hurt less than the bullets would if they hit her, and she knew rope burns like that would heal in no time.

When she reached the bottom of the rope she spun, smiled at the sight of the shocked fighters below as she let go, and transformed into her wolf form before she hit the ground and rolled.

She came up with a growl and took down the first shooter

right away. All of the fighters turned their attention on her and, like clockwork, the airship dropped as it let out hot air. More men and women appeared on the ropes above, but these fighters were too focused on the large wolf tearing through them to see the approaching danger.

BAM! A shot took out her next victim, and she turned to see William there, rifle now turning to another.

BAM! The other one fell.

With the thrill of the fight coursing through her veins, Cammie ran on all fours toward the large man at the rear of the compound. He stood there with a shotgun in one hand, a grenade in the other.

The first shot sent buckshot through her and it hurt like hell, but it wasn't silver. She pushed forward, knocking the shotgun away.

He backed up, pulling the pin of the grenade, eyes on the ship.

No way was that happening.

She tore a chunk out of his thigh with her teeth and then dropped it as she transformed back into herself, turning to snatch the grenade away and slam it into his mouth with all her Were strength. It shattered teeth and with the assistance of an elbow to lodge it in place, was stuck.

Not wanting to feel the burn of its shrapnel, she dropped and spun, kicking his legs out from under him and then catching them with hers to twist him so that he fell face-first. Next she transformed and ran away as fast as she could until—

KA-BOOM!

The blast sent her sprawling forward, but she was unharmed. When she stood, turning back to see what had happened, all she saw was red on the compound doors and ground. The lump of his body that remained was just nasty, not worth a second glance.

His followers were in shock, and one after another were cut down or shot. Cammie's companions knew their role. These people hadn't come over willingly, and they weren't in the habit of creating prisons on the island.

When it was done, Cammie found her clothes where they had fallen during her descent from the ship, dressed, and waved everyone to her.

They gathered around her, not a single one of them injured.

"That's how the fuck we do business," Cammie shouted.

They replied with a war-cry-style cheer.

She looked around at the carnage, then continued, "Our work here is done for now. Let's get home and take a well-earned vacation. You with me?"

Again they cheered, and then headed for the gate as the ship touched down just outside it so they wouldn't have to climb back up the ropes.

When they were all back aboard, Bertha and the others looked at Cammie with wide, terrified eyes.

"Oh, you didn't hear the part about me being a Werewolf?" Cammie asked.

Bertha nodded. "We heard, just...never had any reason to believe in horror stories."

"Think of it more like a superhero story." Cammie let her claws grow and eyes flash yellow as she told them, "These are my superpowers, and I'm here to save the world."

"Vampires?" the man beside Bertha asked. "Demons, necromancers, all that stuff is real too? How about dragons? Armies of the dead, like zombies and whatnot?"

Cammie laughed. "Vampires, yes. But again, the ones *I* know are on the side of justice. They're good, just like you all, though there are good and bad. The rest of it is all hogwash."

"That you know of." The man gave a doubtful look at the others around him. "For all I know, any one of you could be a shapeshifter and sprout dragon wings out of your back at any minute."

Bertha whacked up him upside the head. "Shut up, you're going to give me nightmares."

"What? I'm just saying that if a Werewolf's real, anything could be."

"And I'm saying don't fill my mind with that garbage. I'll just keep on believing only what my eyes see and nothing more."

Cammie smiled, finding herself enjoying their bickering for some reason. Then it hit her—a memory of her own parents fighting like this long ago. Of course, the topic then had been something simple like what to eat for dinner, but the tone was the same.

It was followed by a quick flash of a memory, one of her dad rocking her to sleep as he sang a song…something like "Coombaya Milo." She laughed at the memory, more of a pleasant nostalgic chuckle really, and then turned to march into the control room.

William was at the controls, starting to turn the ship around already.

"We're really done out here?" he asked. "For now, I mean?"

She nodded. "The immediate area is secure."

He continued to steer for a moment, but she noticed his sideways glance at her.

"What is it?"

"Just… I heard you and Royland talking." He lifted the control to take the ship to a higher altitude, then set the course before turning to face her. "About the boy, Kristof. You going to take him home?"

She nodded.

"Meaning…" He frowned, as if saying this next part was incredibly difficult. "Meaning, you're leaving us."

"In good hands, I assure you."

He shook his head, unable to accept that. "There's nobody on that island I trust as much as you. Nobody who could corral the people like you have."

"I think there's one," she replied with a smile.

"No, I..." He paused, mouth open, then frowned. "Me?"

"I've seen the way they look at you. Maybe they fear me, maybe they love me, I don't know. But they follow you because you're one of them."

He leaned against the controls, accidentally hitting the altitude control so that the ship dipped slightly before he corrected it.

"Well, damn."

"Damn as in you accept?"

He laughed. "Damn, as in I hate to see you go but I'm incredibly honored by your trust in me."

"You'll do well, because you're honorable."

"Don't forget that I was a pirate."

"I've learned that not all pirates were *actually* pirates." She stood to join the rest of her crew. "But that said, if I ever come back and find out you've let the old ways return, we will have a problem."

"Noted, and not something to worry about."

She nodded, then left him to captain the ship.

For the rest of the journey, Cammie got to know their new companions. Bertha was quite the fun one to be around, so much so that when they were preparing to land Cammie told her she was going to do her best to get Bertha a place next to their own.

"I thought you were heading east, across the ocean?" Bertha asked, repeating the information that Cammie had conveyed during their conversation.

"True, but we'll be back before you know it, and I'll need a woman to chat with. We can compare stories about these goofballs." She nodded to Bertha's man, and he smirked. "The stories Bertha has to share would make you cringe, girl."

Cammie laughed. "You clearly don't know me at all."

The community at Prince Edward Island was thriving. In just a short time they had managed to give it a festive feel, so that it looked almost like a tourist attraction compared to the compound Bertha and her crew had come from.

Flags of various colors flapped in the wind and one of the women had taken to carving wood, so that part of the streets now showed off wooden sculptures or reliefs of ships, airships, wolves, and more.

They even had tiki torches and fire pits on the beach so that each evening would be a celebration of life.

That's what they had here, Cammie thought as she smiled, happy to be home and see it all again. A new life.

Royland had been hard at work setting up security including walls and watch towers, both on the mainland and on the island. He had also had the community work on providing equal housing for all residents. With all of the newcomers arriving thanks to Cammie's work, he had invited many of the older residents into the main hotel, which the Prince had once occupied.

After introducing the newcomers to the team that handled processing and finding them quarters, Cammie made her way home.

She paused out front, watching Kristof and the dog, whom the boy had named Elroy, wrestling over a stick. Finally the boy broke it free and pulled it back to throw, then turned and ran instead.

Elroy chased after him, her tongue hanging out in pure joy.

There was something about all this that made her very happy, a feeling of calm that said this was the life.

But another part of her said it couldn't last. She knew it was true and didn't fight it, but instead focused on appreciating the moment. Soon they would take the boy home, maybe work to address the pirate issue over there, and she hoped that Valerie would go along for the ride.

Kristof finally saw her, threw the stick, and ran over to give her a hug.

"All went well?" he asked.

"We have new friends and fewer enemies." She ruffled his hair, beaming. "What else could we ask for?"

She had meant that statement to purely refer to the trip, but instantly his expression darkened and she knew he was thinking about his family. That's what else he could hope for, and she felt like an idiot for making him think it.

Elroy came bounding back, stick in her mouth, and Kristof's smile returned as he returned to playing with the dog.

Cammie went inside and sat beside the bed where Royland was sleeping. She couldn't take her eyes off of him, this man who had totally made her rethink the way she saw relationships—the world, even. And she hoped she had done the same for him.

He was here at her side, day and night. Well, during the day he couldn't always be at her side, but he did what he could when he could.

She wanted to tell him about their recent journey but also knew he needed sleep, so she curled up next to him and joined him in slumber.

When she woke, she first turned to the window to see the sun setting, then to the boy, Kristof, sleeping on the couch with the dog at his side. A motion caused her to jump, and only then did she realize Royland wasn't next to her.

He was stepping out of the bathroom, towel wrapped around his waist and hair still damp.

"We can't wait," he commented, nodding at Kristof. "The boy has already waited long enough."

Cammie nodded, pulling her knees to her chest on the bed. "Agreed."

"You wanted to wait for Val, but…"

"She would have been here by now?" Cammie shook her head, agreeing. "She had her agenda, her goals. Either she's still searching for Robin's parents, or taking down Toro, or has headed off to her next task. We don't fit into that equation anymore."

Royland slowly nodded. "Tomorrow, then. The ship will be ready?"

"Yes, but not William."

It only took a second for Royland to figure out what that meant, and he smiled at the thought. "Good choice, that one. He'll make a fine leader."

"Temporary leader," she corrected. "We're coming back."

"I hope so too," he replied. "But I am more skeptical than you."

The next morning came quickly enough, and soon they had the ship loaded. Reems would be captaining the ship, the same captain who had led the first successful trade mission with New York since the pirates had gone clean.

Kristof and Elroy were below decks, getting settled in and keeping Royland company since he couldn't come out into the sun. Cammie had finished saying farewell to everyone, so she went to the control room and nodded to Reems.

"You know that comm device?" Cammie asked.

He nodded. "Get in contact with them yet?"

"Naw, I mean, they said it was for Valerie." Cammie took it from her pack and held it in front of her, amazed at the little buttons and solar charging glass. "This kind of technology, it's almost like magic to me. Might as well be."

"If it actually works."

"Well, that's what I was thinking we'd find out." She smiled. "Seeing as Valerie's not back and we don't know if she's even coming back this way, I thought I'd let New York know."

The captain perked up, pausing in his flight-check duties to turn her way. "Well then, what're we waiting for?"

She nodded, then flipped the power switch. After playing with it for a moment there were a few beeps, followed by a static sound and then a voice.

"Hello? Val?" a man's voice asked, followed by a couple of excited voices and then Sandra's, "Is that you?"

"Sorry to disappoint everyone," Cammie stated. "Just Cammie here."

"Holy shit!" Sandra laughed. "It's good to hear your voice, Cammie. What's going on? Val's hasn't returned from Toro?"

Cammie's gut clenched as she thought about how to say it. "The thing is, she never said for sure she *would* be back. And... we're leaving."

"Leaving for where?"

"We have pirates to face on the other side of the ocean, and a boy to take home. The island is in good hands, but we just—"

"Cammie!" Captain Reems hissed.

She held up a hand to tell him to wait, but when she glanced up she froze, seeing what he was staring at. Airships on the horizon, several of them, coming their way.

"Uh, guys..."

"Yes?" Sandra's voice came through, worried.

"Either we're under attack and the Prince won, or Valerie just came back."

"Judging by that carving on the side of the main ship," Captain Reems chimed in as he stared through military-grade binoculars, "I'd say it's your friend Valerie."

Cammie handed him the radio, ignoring the questions coming from the other side, and had a look. Sure enough, the lead ship had a large carving of a vampire skull over crossbones, bat-like wings coming out of the skull.

"That'd be Valerie," Cammie agreed with a chuckle. She grabbed the radio back and told them, "Our departure has been delayed due to the unexpected return of the Vampire Princess. We'll call when she's landed."

Cheers erupted from the other side and Sandra warned, "You

tell her that if she doesn't call right away, she'll answer to me. And you do *not* want to piss off a pregnant lady. I don't care how powerful of a vampire you are."

She signed off and headed below deck to tell Royland the good news, heart still thumping at the crazy timing of it all.

CHAPTER TWENTY-THREE

Prince Edward Island

When her ship landed on the field at Prince Edward Island, the former pirates were already gathering around. In the lead was Cammie, a small boy and a dog next to her.

"Was I gone so long?" Valerie called as she waited for the gangplank to be lowered. "You two had enough time to have a child and get a dog?"

Cammie laughed and stepped forward to greet her at the bottom of the gangplank with a hug. "You were gone a while, but not that long."

A glance past Cammie showed one ship looking like it was about to set off, and Valerie sensed unease coming from the Were.

"You going somewhere?" Valerie asked.

"To take this boy home," Cammie replied. "That, and maybe deal with some European pirates along the way."

"I hear they don't call themselves pirates over there."

"So you've heard of them?" Cammie's eyes went wide. "You aren't just returning, you were going to sail over there and deal with them."

"It seems we might've met out there if not here, at any rate." Valerie looked at her ships, thinking that they were all set for sailing.

"There's something I wanted to show you," Cammie said, excitement glistening in her eyes. "Come on."

As they walked back to Cammie's ship, she glanced at the other ships as if just realizing that Robin wasn't there.

"She...didn't come back?"

Valerie shook her head, and that was enough. As soon they were on the ship Royland greeting her with a hug, and then they made for the control room.

"Close your eyes," Cammie said.

"What?" Valerie laughed. "No way am I doing that."

"Come on, you're a super-powerful vampire who can smell trouble coming from a mile away. Just close your damn eyes."

Valerie rolled her eyes, and then closed them. "Okay, what now?"

A clicking sounded, followed by a voice she never expected.

"Cammie?" Sandra's voice said, crackling. "Is she there?"

Valerie was overjoyed, eyes bursting open as she darted forward and took the odd-looking metal box from Cammie.

"No way. Sandra?"

"Dammit, Val! Took you long enough." Sandra sounded like she was caught between laughing and crying. "How the hell have you been?"

"We're fine, and have tales to tell," Valerie answered. "What's going on there?"

"New York's held together. At times on a thin string, but we're managing."

"And the baby? Everything looks healthy with the pregnancy?"

"She's definitely showing," Diego cut in, slightly muffled. "Ouch!" He laughed. "In a good way, in a *VERY* good way."

"Damn right," Sandra agreed. "Val, we miss you. And if you're not here for the birth of my baby, I will hunt you down and kick your ass. Got it?"

Valerie laughed. "I'll do my best." A long silence followed, then she added, "Looks like we have business across the ocean. Time to get my tourist on."

"Yeah, so I heard." Sandra paused, then asked, "Val, when's it over? Are you ever really coming home?"

Valerie thought about that, looking from the comm device to Cammie and then to the west, refusing to linger on thoughts of Robin and Toronto. Valerie had accomplished so much, but still had so much left to do. She would get everyone situated who wanted to stay and then the rest would sail across the ocean with them to continue the fight.

"Home, Sandra? Earth is my home, for now. And until it's safe for us all, this is where I belong. Out here, fighting for justice."

THE END

AUTHOR NOTES - JUSTIN SLOAN

WRITTEN JULY 31, 2017

Life is crazy. I should have gotten this book to you a week earlier (well, because of cover artist timing and all that, it would have been impossible anyway, but at least I would have been done). Some of you already know what happened, but for those of you not on my author newsletter or the Reclaiming Honor Facebook page, here it is:

This is literally the first book I have bled over to get to you.

That's right, I sacrificed my life (kinda) to finish this book. The not too long version of the story is that I was writing the last two chapters at a café, thinking I would finish it up and then head over to the gym for a celebratory workout, when someone runs in, grabs my laptop right out from under me, and takes off.

It took me a second to process this, and I even thought about just letting him have it. That thought vanished as soon as I realized my Dropbox was full and the book wasn't backed up—meaning, I wasn't sure I'd ever finish the book. Trying to rewrite material is grueling, and I don't know... So yeah, that all went through my head and then I stood and took off after him. I caught up to him just outside, as he was trying to get into the car.

He had a getaway driver waiting, so he was climbing into the passenger side, but had the computer toward me. Idiot.

I grabbed the computer and we struggled, but then the lady started driving. She was shouting at me to get out of the car, some punches were thrown, and then they pulled into the street. Finally, I wrestled the computer away (or he let go? I can't remember) and went rolling across the road. The car behind us stopped, thankfully.

So yeah, I recovered my computer, but lost my glasses. I had to get four stitches in my lip and had a bunch of bruises, but that was all.

Not so bad, right? But a crazy day for me, nonetheless, and one I hope *not* to repeat anytime soon.

The happy ending to that story is that a couple days later I finally finished this book that you have before you, and am getting ready to start on the next one. We have amazing things planned with Craig Martelle and others with PT Hylton, and this universe is going to keep expanding in unimaginable ways.

In my non Kurtherian Gambit Universe (KGU) writing, I've had a lot of fun lately too. I launched a Space Marine / Time Travel series with two other writers, and we've brought in three other writers to do an anthology in that series and then spinoffs, similar to what we're doing here with KGU, but without vampires and all that. It might have some magic though! I've always loved the idea of scifi fantasy, but understand the need to keep it from getting carried away. Therefore, that series (Syndicate Wars) keeps it very much to a minimum.

However, I'm doing a solo spinoff from there, with the idea that I'll go full steam ahead on the magic in space stuff – so be on the lookout! I have an awesome artist working on the covers as we speak.

On the note of covers, I'd love to hear what you all think of the new direction we took on the covers for these Reclaiming Honor books. We're going for more of a personal connection, up close on Valerie, with brighter colors too so they stand out on Amazon. We really hope you like them, because I spent many hours going through artist websites and finding styles that could work and then contacting the artists, etc.

It's not easy, but hey, that's why we get paid, right?

On that note, this was my first real month being fulltime. Guess what? It's also a new record for how much my books have made! It probably helps that I released four books in just one week not long ago, haha, and have more coming down the pipeline. Not every series is a success, and it's always interesting to watch these books launch and see what the fan reaction is.

For example, Reclaiming Honor has, as you've probably guessed, been a huge success. But book five (Born into Flames) had some very mixed reviews. There were a lot of people emailing me or saying in reviews that it was their favorite book in the series by far, and almost as many people saying the opposite. Funny how that works, huh? I hope the ending of this book doesn't cause similar reactions, but here's the thing... TRUST US! Please...? Haha. The way we have it outlined is really cool, and a lot of the complaints I hear from people are already addressed—just a couple books out, sometimes.

Much like the complaints about the Age of Magic, and readers not seeing how they fit in to the world. That's what we think makes it fun. Eventually you'll get to the moment where you do see it, where it all comes together for you, and you'll be like DAMMMNNN! THAT WAS AWESOME!

We hope.

In the meantime, thanks for all the amazing reviews and feedback. We love your personal notes and really feel like we're in a literary version of Cheers, you know? People like Alastar and Kelly, Theresa, Robin, and so many others (sorry for not naming all of you, I'm just getting these author notes down and just letting the fingers take over – I greatly appreciate you!). You all make the difference. Sharing a snippet is like walking into the bar in cheers, and then you all reply with your version of "Norm!" which to us is likes on Facebook, comments, etc.

So once again, thank you so much for that. You make the difference. You keep us writing. (Well, okay, we love writing and would probably do it even if only our moms read it, but wouldn't write with as much passion).

Back to writing the next book. Take care!

AUTHOR NOTES - MICHAEL ANDERLE

AUGUST 6TH, 2017

First, THANK YOU for not only reading this book, but making it all of the way to the end, and reading these author notes, as well!

There isn't as much to say about the series, and Justin's laptop response since he took care of it. Nor, thankfully, do I have to accuse him of Author Note Blocking me like I did PT Hylton and CM Raymond where they put links to video's in their Author Notes, causing others to skip RIGHT out of the book, and ignore anything behind the video link.

Like, my Author Notes ;-)

I'm writing these notes from the Omni Hotel in San Diego, California. It's 2:05 AM here and tonight, my younger brother (9 years) and I are going to see Metallica at the baseball stadium next door. Before that, we are meeting my brother and brother-in-law for a sailing adventure.

I pray I don't get sea sick, cause that would right piss me off. I wouldn't blame anyone but myself, but 'boy howdy' would I give myself a pretty stern talking to and I would deserve it.

Because apparently, I would be an authentic *wuss*. That I even think it could happen is rather embarrassing to admit.

So, last night my brother and I go out to eat a steak dinner. The concierge tells us about Graystone, and off we go to walk the streets of the Gas Lamp District in San Diego.

Now, almost every time before this, I've only been out and about during the day. The Gas Lamp District isn't that impressive during weekdays. So, I wasn't expecting much at night.

Holy CRAP was I wrong. The party is *definitely* after the sun goes down.

Any-hooo, we walk the eight blocks to the steakhouse, get a seat (upstairs by the rail, if you know the restaurant) and get the menus.

Two for food, one for drinks.

I look at the drink menu and set it down. It was all alcohol and they serve Coke.

Decision made.

Now, it was time to decide on the meat and our waiter was spouting on about their Wagyu meat (Japanese, American, and Australian). I'm a Filet Mignon kind of man because I love meat, and not so much the fat. I'll take an eight-ounce Filet over a sixteen-ounce strip or t-bone any day.

But, Wagyu is supposed to be the most exquisite steak in the world complete with the prices to confirm it. At $22 AN OUNCE, I've hesitated to even try it.

But, my brother was willing. So, a polite request for the *minimum* serving size later (6 ounces, if you are curious) we are served this steak, cut up on a plate and before my brother is fully aware of the plates on the table, I had already speared a piece and started chewing.

It's…ok. The fat content is too high for me to really enjoy it so after another three or four bites, I gave the rest to him and requested a filet.

However, bucket list item accomplished, I've had Wagyu Beef from Japan and that was made possible because YOU fans love the Kurtherian Gambit and keep telling friends about the stories.

From the bottom of my heart (and stomach), thank you for all of your support for Kurtherian Gambit, Oriceran and the other authors!

Metallica wouldn't be nearly as possible without you.

Michael

BOOKS BY JUSTIN SLOAN

SCIENCE FICTION

RECLAIMING HONOR (Vampires and Werewolves - Kurtherian Gambit Universe)

Justice is Calling

Claimed by Honor

Judgment has Fallen

Angel of Reckoning

Born into Flames

Defending the Lost

Return of Victory

Shadow Corps (Space Opera Fantasy - Seppukarian Universe)

Shadow Corps

Shadow Worlds

Shadow Fleet

War Wolves (Space Opera Fantasy - Seppukarian Universe)

Bring the Thunder

Click Click Boom

Light Em Up

Syndicate Wars (Space Marines and Time Travel - Seppukarian Universe)

First Strike

The Resistance

Fault Line

False Dawn

Empire Rising

FANTASY

The Hidden Magic Chronicles (Epic Fantasy - Kurtherian Gambit Universe)

Shades of Light

Shades of Dark

Shades of Glory

Shades of Justice

FALLS OF REDEMPTION (Epic Fantasy Series)

Land of Gods

Retribution Calls

Tears of Devotion

MODERN NECROMANCY (Supernatural Thriller)

Death Marked

Death Bound

Death Crowned

CURSED NIGHT (Supernatural Thriller with Werewolves and Vampires)

Hounds of God

Hounds of Light

Hounds of Blood (2018)

ALLIE STROM (MG Urban Fantasy Trilogy)

Allie Strom and the Ring of Solomon

Allie Strom and the Sword of the Spirit

Allie Strom and the Tenth Worthy

BOOKS BY MICHAEL ANDERLE

For a complete list of books by Michael Anderle, please visit:

www.lmbpn.com/ma-books/

All LMBPN Audiobooks are Available at Audible.com and iTunes. For a complete list of audiobooks visit:

www.lmbpn.com/audible

CONNECT WITH THE AUTHORS

Justin Sloan Social

For a chance to see ALL of Justin's different Book Series Check out his website below!

Website: http://JustinSloanAuthor.com

Email List: http://JustinSloanAuthor.com/Newsletter

Facebook Here:
https://www.facebook.com/JustinSloanAuthor

Michael Anderle Social

Website:
http://kurtherianbooks.com/

Email List:
http://kurtherianbooks.com/email-list/

Facebook Here:
https://www.facebook.com/TheKurtherianGambitBooks/

Made in the USA
Las Vegas, NV
16 February 2021